3013: SCARRED

BOOKS IN THE 3013 SERIES:
(IN ORDER PUBLISHED)

NOVELLAS

3013: SCARRED

A 3013 NOVELLA

SUSAN HAYES

DEDICATION

This story is dedicated to everyone who bears the scars of the past on their skin or in their hearts. Wear them with pride. They are signs of strength and reminders of what you have already survived.

And as always, my thanks go to my parents for believing in me, and to Karen, for her unwavering friendship, support, and a decade's worth of laughter.

PROLOGUE

THE YEAR IS 3013.

Earth barely survived the Alien Wars that have ravaged the planet, and an unknown virus had nearly wiped out the entire population. On the brink of extinction, humans struggle to rebuild their civilization, although nothing would ever bring back what once was.

Enforcing martial law, a new age of mankind is born, where warriors rule and women are the ultimate prize. Only the elite earn breeding rights and are granted leave to claim a woman in pairs. Men dream of the day that they will be able to claim a woman to love, but for those chosen being claimed means the end of their freedom and a beginning to a lifelong bond with two strangers. The warriors may have the choice, but the battle for their woman's heart has only begun…

CHAPTER ONE

LAESA FEN HUMMED TO HERSELF AS HER BRUSH FLEW across the canvas. She was trying to capture one of her childhood memories—watching one of Tartarus' many storms roll in from beyond the mountains that surrounded her family home. She could still recall the way the black clouds would blot out the dark red sky as the rumble of thunder grew louder with the passing seconds. She had spent hours watching the storms rage outside her bedroom window as a girl. She'd loved the way the red lightning danced and flashed overhead. The brilliant explosions of light and color and the constant roiling motion of the clouds had held her rapt for hours.

Even as a girl she'd been fascinated by light and colors. Her parents had always known she'd be an artist one day. They'd supported and encouraged her every day of their lives. Lives that were cut short when a Lord broke the treaty with his neighbor and invaded the valley Laesa and her family called home.

Their deaths had happened more than a year ago, now. Enough time had passed that the memories of that night no longer tore at her soul, but Laesa doubted she would ever be able to think of her parents without a pang of grief and loss. Time healed all wounds, but the scars left behind were a permanent reminder of what she'd survived, and what she'd lost.

The dark memories killed her creativity, and left her staring at the canvas. She set down her brush with reluctance, but she knew better than to force herself to continue when her mind wasn't on her work. The painting would suffer for it. Besides, her shoulders ached, and she'd been sitting still so long parts of her lower body had gone completely numb. It was time for a break.

She checked the time and winced. She'd sat down to paint almost five hours ago. Time had gotten away from her again. She needed to get out of her chair, stretch, and find something to eat. At least obtaining sustenance would not be difficult. The shopping area of the newly established Alliance Station: X21 was far from full, but there were several food vendors set up to provide meals to the ones who lived and worked onboard.

Her favorite restaurant of all happened to be located right next door to her temporary gallery and workspace. She'd gotten permission from the station's Commander, Olivia Jacobson, to unofficially occupy a vacant store on a short term basis. It gave her a place to store her art supplies, and she'd managed to create a small but well-lit studio at the back. She'd come here to paint a single mural on the wall of a friend's new business, but others had seen her work and hired her to do various projects, including a few commissions and portraits.

On the way out, she stopped to rearrange the paintings she had on display. Landscapes mostly, images of Tartarus, her home world. She hadn't expected people to be so intrigued by the planet she'd left behind. To Laesa, it was simply home, with nothing extraordinary about it.

To others though, it was a place of legend. After years of being nearly inaccessible to off-worlders, Tartarus had become a mystery, a place only a few had ever visited. Her paintings were the first images many of her visitors had seen of her planet, and their curiosity drew them in. It was ironic that she'd left Tartarus months ago in order to escape her past only to sell paintings of her home world in order to afford her new life.

The universe was not without a sense of humor.

She walked to the doorway and took a moment to enjoy the view. The station was so new that everything still gleamed. Alliance Station: X21 was primarily populated by Alliance personnel at the moment, but there were Krytos on the station, too. They made their home in Asylum, the bar and Krytos sanctuary on the far side of the shopping area. She could see a pair of Krytos males outside the sanctuary doors at that moment and recognized them as Zade and Axton, the owners of Asylum. While she'd never actually been introduced to the brothers, they were impossible to miss with their massive size and powerful presence.

Laesa liked the Krytos she'd met so far, though they'd frightened her at first because they reminded her of

Tarin males. As she'd gotten to know them, she'd come to understand that the Krytos were very different from the males of her species. They were both fierce warrior-races, but that was where the similarities ended. Krytos males generally treated their females as equals, while many Tarin males considered the females of their species to be weak and inconsequential outside the bedchamber.

After spending several nightmarish months as a harem slave owned by a Tarin warlord, Laesa was painfully aware of how little regard some males had for the females under their care. Recently change had come to Tartarus, the result of a civil war that had finally put an end to the old ways. Because of that war, females who had been enslaved were now free. Many Tarin females had chosen to leave their home world and seek a new, better life for themselves elsewhere, just as Laesa had done.

"Hey, Laesa. I was about to come in and drag you next door for something to eat," a cheerful voice announced.

Laesa turned and smiled down at her human friend, Sophie. "Good day, Sophie. There is no need for you to drag me anywhere. I was on my way to your restaurant to buy something to eat. Not that you could have truly dragged me anywhere. I am far too big for you to do that."

The petite blonde shrugged her shoulders. "You have a point there. You're so tall...and all those curves. There was a time I would have been jealous of you, you know. You're gorgeous."

"As are you, Sophie. An opinion I know your bonded would agree with. One day, I am going to get you to sit for me so I can paint your portrait. Then you will see what I see when I look at you."

Sophie started to shake her head in refusal, then stopped. "Do you think Jake and Dan would like that? I mean, if you did it, and I gave it to them as a gift? Our anniversary is coming up next month and I have no idea what to give them." She lifted a hand to her face, touching the star marking beside her eye. "Could you paint me without this?"

Laesa nodded. "I believe they would like that, yes. I would be honored to create such a gift for you. And I could leave your marking off if you wish me to. You're lovely with or without it, my friend." Laesa knew the star tattoo Sophie wore bothered her. It was a stark, permanent reminder that Sophie was infertile. Among the Alliance's female population, the mark was common, though in Sophie's case it had not prevented her from being claimed by a pair of Alliance elites who loved their chosen without reservation.

Sophie beamed with delight, her emotional response strong enough to make her personal energy field surge for a moment. Like all Tarins, Laesa could sense a little of an individual's energy. As an artist, she translated what she sensed into light and colors, and worked them into her portraits, imbuing her paintings with traces of her subject's energy. When she looked at Sophie, she could sometimes see hints of the female's warmth and kindness. It would be a pleasure to be able to show Sophie that part of herself.

"We'll talk details later, but thank you! And not a word to the guys, okay? I'm going to surprise them."

Laesa nodded. "They will not hear of this from me. You have my word."

Sophie threw her arms around Laesa and hugged her with surprising strength considering her size. "Thank you so much! Oh, I'm so excited. I have to pick out something to wear. Maybe that dress they like, the blue one. And my hair, what am I going to do with my hair?"

Laesa returned her friend's hug and laughed. Sophie's exuberance was contagious, and Laesa was happy to have the female's friendship. "You know you should wear it down. I have heard them say many times that they like it that way."

"So true. They really are opinionated, aren't they? It's a good thing I love them, or I'd have throttled them by now. C'mon, I came over here because I know you must be starving. I set aside some of my lasagna for you. I know that's your favorite."

"You are an excellent cook, Sophie. I like everything you prepare, but it is possible that lasagna is my favorite. It reminds me of a dish my mother used to make."

Sophie perked up, her eyes alight with interest. "Is that so? Do you know how to make it? I could always use a new recipe, and so far, I don't have any Tarin dishes on the menu."

"I would be happy to tell you how to make it, but if you want to prepare Tarin food, you are going to need more spices. I'll prepare a list for you while I eat."

"No, you won't. You're going to eat and relax. You work too hard, Laesa. You've been looking tired lately. Are you sleeping enough?"

Laesa activated a program on her wrist unit that would alert her if anyone entered her workspace. The device been a gift from Sophie and her bonded. They'd presented it to her not long after they'd become friends. Laesa cherished it, as both a powerful piece of technology and as a token of friendship from her first non-Tarin friend.

After securing the shop, she let herself be led into Sophie's café as her friend continued to express her concern about Laesa's well-being.

The truth was that no amount of sleep would solve her tiredness. Laesa knew what the problem was, but she wasn't ready to address it yet. Tarins ate and drank like other beings, but to remain strong and healthy, they needed to consume energy, as well. Usually, they fed off the energy of a sexual release. They could feed off of bloodlust and battle frenzy as well, but Laesa was no warrior. She'd been raised to be an artist, and the females of her race were no longer trained to fight the way they'd once been.

That left her with only one way to feed, and after her time as a harem slave, she was reluctant to do so. In fact, she had postponed her next feeding for longer than she should have. Soon, she would have to give in to her body's demands and choose a partner to feed from. At least she could now choose who she laid with.

It was a freedom she would never take for granted again.

Rhen Torven walked half a pace in front of his twin brother, Sabar, as they made their way across the station's shopping area. They'd finalized the last few details required to officially lease space in the brand new station's cargo bays, and some office space to go with it. It had taken a few favors, all their charm, and some good luck, but they'd managed to get the space they needed despite the Alliance's concerns about having civilian businesses onboard what was technically a military base. At least, it was for now.

While the station was not a hub of commerce yet, they wanted to establish an early presence in the area. One day, relations between the Alliance and the newly discovered Xenon race would improve enough that trade would begin. When that day came, they would be ready.

This new expansion was a milestone accomplishment for their trading company. The two of them had started out with nothing but a few crates of goods from their home planet of Helix, and a lot of determination. After years of work and more than a little good fortune, they had a booming business buying and selling goods from a variety of worlds and cultures, along with a small fleet of ships dedicated to transporting their product anywhere it needed to go.

Life was good, and it was time to do a little celebrating.

"We really did it," Sabar said, grinning.

"We really did. Now we need to organize the business side of things. Set up a small office, bring in a manager to live here and oversee things. You sure you don't want to stay here and run it yourself?" Rhen asked.

"And escape having you as my roommate? Believe me, I considered it." Sabar said with a smirk.

"I'm sorry, I've forgotten. Remind me again which one of us left a half-eaten meal in their quarters so long it set off the bio-hazard warning?" Rhen retorted.

His brother merely glowered at him. "Stupid thing malfunctioned. A little mold never killed anyone."

"Comments like that are why I'm grateful we have a chef and a top of the line food console onboard to save me from your cooking. And while we're here, we've got other options, too." Rhen gestured around them.

"Mhmm. Plenty of choices in food, drink, and pretty females. So many lovely creatures who have yet to have the pleasure of my company," Sabar said.

"The poor, deprived things," Rhen replied with droll humor. The truth was that neither of them had much time for socializing outside of work. Torven Traders had been the focus of both their lives for years now. Despite the fact they had finally reached a point where they could leave more of the day-to-day decisions to their highly talented staff, neither brother had slowed down much. It wasn't in their nature.

In the few days they'd been on the station, neither of them had spent much time in the shopping area. There had been too many other things to do. They'd passed through it, but this was the first time Rhen had taken the time to look around. The stores were mostly vacant spaces, but there were a few shops selling a variety of goods and services, and he made a mental note to track down a list of vendors. Each and every one of them were potential clients, and he had no intention of letting his competitors get to them first. They'd only learned about the Xenon and X21's new destination by sheer luck and a few well-placed connections. It gave them an advantage Rhen wouldn't squander.

A flash of red caught his eye, and he turned to get a better look. Paintings? He pointed out the small display of artwork to his brother. "Do you see what I see, brother? I think those landscapes are of Tartarus."

"Really?" Sabar turned to look in the direction Rhen was pointing. "You might be right. Never seen anything like that before."

"Me either. I think we should delay our celebratory drink to take a closer look. Agreed?"

Sabar nodded. "Agreed. I know better than to argue with your hunches, even though you know as much about art as I do about astronavigation."

Rhen shrugged. "I don't need to know art. If it looks good up close, and the artist is actually Tarin and not merely painting copies of existing images, then we'll have no trouble finding buyers."

"*If* we can talk them into partnering up with us. Do you remember the last time we made an offer to a Tarin? What they consider a friendly negotiation is what some cultures consider a capital crime," Sabar said.

"You're exaggerating."

"As I recall, I was also bleeding by the time it was over."

Rhen rolled his eyes at his brother's dramatics. "That was your own damn fault. You shouldn't have dropped your guard. Mother would have been ashamed of your showing that day. She taught you to fight better than that."

"Next time we're sparring, I'm going to make you eat those words," Sabar muttered under his breath as he straightened the sleeve of his shirt with an irritated tug.

Normally, the two of them preferred to wear more comfortable garb. Loose fitting shirts at least, or better yet, their people's traditional outfit of sleeveless vests with leather pants. In deference to their meeting with the Alliance officials, today they were both wearing human-style clothing. Crisp, white shirts with cuffs and collars that made Rhen feel confined. He knew Sabar felt the same. Once they were finished checking out the paintings, they should probably head back to their ship to change before going to celebrate.

Sabar was ready to indulge in a night of relaxation and fun. He and his twin were overdue for some downtime. As far as he was concerned, there was no point in working their tails off to fill their accounts with credits if they never took the time to spend them. It wasn't like they could take it with them when they died. Now that the deals were done and they were established on X21, he wanted to take the time to explore a little.

They approached the paintings, and Rhen went straight to the nearest one while Sabar went looking for the owner. He had to be nearby. "Hello?" Sabar called out as he walked the length of the small gallery. He received no answer.

The far back of the somewhat cluttered space had been converted into an artist's studio. It was well-lit and there was an incomplete painting set up on the easel. He moved in closer to take a better look. As he did, a delicious scent tickled his nose. It was both familiar and strange at the same time, and he drew in a deeper breath, trying to identify it. It was too faint, though he felt a strange stirring in his blood as he caught a trace of the scent again.

Still puzzled, he turned to go and spotted a tall, beautiful Tarin female in her mid-twenties entering the shop. She was dressed in a flowing black skirt that swirled around her long legs, and her top was a nearly shapeless thing of mottled shades of gray that stole some of the luster from her golden skin. Her straight black hair fell to the line of her jaw, which was shorter than he'd ever seen on a female of her species.

Not that he'd seen many Tarin females. Most of them never left Tartarus. The few he'd seen had been concubines traveling with their masters. He'd heard rumors that things were changing on the Tarin home world, and that the days of keeping harems and taking slaves were over. If that was the case, it would explain why a Tarin female was so far from home without a male nearby.

"Good day to you both. How may I be of service to you?" Her voice was as lovely as her face, and Sabar's pulse kicked up another notch. He moved to join his brother, and as he got closer, the enticing scent he'd picked up in the back returned and grew stronger.

"Good day to you as well. Are these paintings your work? They're remarkable." Sabar was trying to keep his wording formal since he'd noticed that the few Tarins he'd met tended to speak that way, but it was hard to concentrate as the delicious aroma drifted into his lungs. Intoxicating. That's what it was. Like the perfume of night blooming flowers blended with a sultry, spicy note he'd never come across before.

Understanding slammed into him a second later. She was the source of the scent. It wasn't her perfume, it was her.

Holy nova.

Rhen inhaled deeply, and his eyes widened as the truth dawned on him as well. Because they were twins, they'd always known it was likely they would be drawn to the same female. They just never imagined that they could be attracted so strongly to a Tarin.

The female looked at them both with wariness in her black eyes. "I'm Laesa Fen, and yes, these are all my work. Is there something wrong? You both look a little unsettled."

Fuck yes, he was unsettled. Her scent called to him like a beacon in the darkness, and all he wanted to do was get closer to the beautiful female who smelled so tantalizing.

Laesa stood in the middle of the room and tried to slow her rapidly beating heart. Her Helios visitors were the first of their kind she'd seen up close, but it wasn't their size or primal presence that had her off-balance. What had her pulse pounding was the energy that surged around them both. They were attracted to her. Their reaction was so strong, she couldn't help but sense it.

Her first instinct was to move away from them, but she resisted. They had done nothing to warrant her distrust. They were potential customers, not threats. She took a quick breath and banished her worries to the back of her mind.

The male closest to her offered her a smile that showed a flash of his fangs as he answered her previous inquiry. "I'm not unsettled really, merely surprised. You're not what I expected."

"You were expecting a Tarin male, I imagine." Even as she spoke, Laesa couldn't help but admire her two customers. They were tall and well built, not as large as a Tarin or Krytos male, but there was an edge to them both that told her they could be just as dangerous. They had identical features, and she guessed they must be twins. Their amber eyes gleamed with intelligence, and they both wore their hair long and loose around their shoulders, their burnished gold locks highlighted with hints of coppery red. She had a sudden urge to sketch their faces, putting down the lines and angles of their features so she could study them at her leisure.

The other male came in closer, and she watched the way he moved with interest. He had a lethal grace that hinted at the animal within. She didn't know much about the Helios species, but she knew they were a shapeshifting race, able to change from their bipedal form to one of a large, four-legged predator similar to the *venar* of her home world. She had always wanted to see a Helios in their animal form. Now that she'd finally met a Helios, she wasn't sure she wanted that anymore. They were a little overwhelming up close, especially these two.

"You're right, we were expecting a male. I confess that I'm very happy to have been wrong. My name is Sabar Torven, and this is my brother, Rhen. We spotted your paintings and had to come over to take a closer look. Is this really what Tartarus looks like?"

"That is my home, yes. At least, that's how I remember it. Most of the landscapes are of places near where I grew up."

"You're very talented," the one called Rhen said.

"And beautiful," Sabar added, moving in closer still. Before she could put space between them, he had her hand in his and was lifting it to his mouth. He brushed a gentle kiss to the back of her hand, and she felt his energy flow over her skin like a caress. That one small taste awakened her hunger, and reminded her that she would need to feed. Soon.

Sabar felt her fingers tremble as he kissed her, and he forced himself to back off before he went too far. Her scent wrapped around him, tempting him to make a play for her right here and now, but he knew better. There was a delicate trace of fear on the air. Her fear. Something about them scared her, and the last thing in the cosmos he wanted was for this stunning creature to fear him or his brother.

He released her hand with reluctance, and she backed away from him, holding the hand he'd kissed tight against her body. Whatever she'd experienced, it had left her guarded. He and Rhen would have to proceed carefully, and that wasn't something Sabar was very good at. He was more the kind to dive in and ask forgiveness later.

He looked to his brother, who was staring intently at two paintings of people hanging near the back of the room. "Do you do portraits, like these?"

Laesa nodded, clearly happy to be back to the safe topic of her artwork. "I do. Those are commissions awaiting pick-up. I asked permission to display them until then."

Rhen looked thoughtful. "Do you think our parents would like a pair of portraits, Sabar?"

Sabar nodded, impressed with his brother's quick thinking. "I know they would. Laesa, would you be willing to paint us?"

Her gaze darted back and forth between them, but eventually she nodded. "I usually do sittings in my temporary studio, back there." She tipped her head toward the far end of the room. "I think it might be best if you came one at a time. There's not much space."

Rhen was doing his best to stay focused, but it wasn't easy. He was determined, though. He'd seen the way Laesa responded to Sabar's touch. She was interested, but cautious. A little time with each of them in her own space might give them a chance to get to know her better and allow her to get to know them in turn. She was beautiful and alluring, and there was something about her that made him hope that the attraction he was feeling was more than merely physical.

He and Sabar both agreed a long time ago that neither of them would settle for anything but a love match. It was what their parents had, and it was what they wanted, too. They wanted a female who could share every part of their lives. Someone they could life-lock with in a permanent and loving bond that could never be broken. With their business booming and their lives going so well, he and his brother were finally ready to find someone for more than a few nights of mutual pleasure. It was possible they'd just met her.

Only time would tell for sure, but his gut instinct was that she might be the one, and his hunches were rarely wrong.

CHAPTER TWO

LATER, LAESA SAT NEAR THE FRONT OF HER WORKspace, idly sketching as she thought about her newest customers. Rhen and Sabar were nothing like other males she'd met, and she found herself unable to get them out of her mind. They had treated her with respect and consideration, and both of them had been genuinely interested in her artwork. She'd enjoyed speaking with them, and by the time they'd left, she had managed to shed her concerns about their intentions. Their interest in her was still obvious, but they hadn't acted on it. At least, not yet.

She had the sense that neither male was the kind to walk away from something he wanted. They wouldn't be as successful as they were if that was the case, and a quick bit of research after they had left her gallery had made it clear that they were very good at what they did. She hadn't read much, only enough to confirm that they were who they claimed to be.

To check into their lives any further would be intrusive. She had what she needed to know. The rest she could learn from them if they were inclined to share it with her. They'd certainly have time for it. While most artists took three-dimensional scans of their subjects and used those as their model, Laesa preferred to work with her subject in person. She wanted to talk to them, and try to get a sense of their personality so she could incorporate it into her work. Static images worked for basic elements of composition, but it had limitations. She estimated it would take at least several hours with each brother before she had enough of a feel of who they were to finish their portraits properly.

"Hey, you never came back to finish your meal so I brought it over," Sophie announced as she popped into view. "Did your visitors buy anything, or were they just curious?"

"They bought something. Well, they ordered a pair of portraits. I've got the deposit already. Their sittings are all scheduled. One is coming tomorrow and the day after that, and then his brother will sit for me. I am very pleased with their interest in my work."

"That's great! Who is it? Anyone I know?" Sophie asked. She walked up to Laesa and handed her a tray with her re-heated meal, taking the sketchbook in trade.

"They're new to the station. Well, newer than the rest of us," Laesa answered as she settled the tray on her lap and picked up the fork Sophie had included with her meal.

"Holy stars, is this them? They're supernova levels of hot! Are they Helios? They must be with those cat-like eyes."

"Yes, that's them, and yes, they're Helios. They're in shipping and trade. As for their appearance, they do have very nice bone structure, that's why I was sketching them. Painting them will be a pleasure."

"Honey, spending time with either of these two would be a pleasure no matter what you were doing. They're gorgeous, and I'm not talking about bone structure!" Sophie said, still staring at the drawings.

"You're a claimed woman. You're not supposed to say such things. What if your bonded heard you?"

Sophie laughed. "I'm claimed, not blind or dead. I love my boys, but that doesn't mean I can't appreciate another man's appearance. These two are definitely worth appreciating. At least, I think so based on what you've sketched of them. What's with this one's hair?"

Laesa glanced up from her meal to see Sophie pointing to one of her partial drawings of Rhen. "He has strands of white in his hair on one side. I liked the way it looked."

Sophie thumbed through several more pages of new sketches, all of the Torven brothers. "Mhmm. Given the number of times you've drawn these guys, I'd say you liked more than just their hair and bone structure."

Laesa's face burned with embarrassment. "Sophie! They're customers. They have agreed to pay me a handsome fee for their portraits, and I intend to give them my very best work. To do that, I must practice drawing them. That's all. Even if they are handsome, they're not even the same species as I am. And...and...there are two of them!"

Sophie gave her a knowing look, her blue eyes gleaming. "Yes, there are two of them. So, what? You're free now, Laesa. You can live your life however you wish, and with whomever you choose. And believe me, there are advantages to having two men in your life."

"That is true. I mean the part about me having the freedom to live as I wish, not about having two men in my life! Do you know anything about their race? I know they're shifters, but not much else. I suppose I should learn what I can before I meet with them again."

Sophie nodded with such enthusiasm she sent her blonde curls bouncing. "That's a great idea. All I know is that their world is mostly jungle, and they can turn into something that looks like an oversized Earth cat. Big beasts. Oh, and they're a matriarchal society. Which means the women are in charge. Nice idea, isn't it? If you read up tonight, you'll have something to talk about during their sittings. You can ask them about their planet and their lives there. It doesn't matter what race they are, all males love to talk about themselves."

"The women are the leaders? That's very different than back home. Are you sure males prefer to talk about themselves? Today, they asked me many questions about myself. I learned very little about them, save for their names and what they do for a living. They buy and sell goods from all over the galaxy. In fact, they suggested they might be able to help me find buyers for my work."

"They wanted to know about you, huh? Then they're definitely interested, and not just in your artistic talent."

Laesa lowered her gaze to the floor as she made her next confession. "I already knew they were attracted to me. Their energies made that obvious."

Sophie chuckled. "You sensed their emotions? That's cheating! Besides, I thought you couldn't really do that. I still don't understand exactly how your senses work, but you did tell me you couldn't read people's emotions."

Laesa shook her head. "It's hard to explain, and it's not something I can control. It's automatic, like the way you and I hear a sound or experience a flavor or a scent. It's simply that sometimes I get a brief impression of what someone is feeling, especially when there are strong emotions in play. It is never more than a brief impression, though. I'm no mind reader."

"I think it's cool, and I know you would never invade someone's privacy like that, even if you could. You're far too polite to even consider it."

"It would be rude," Laesa agreed. "But, I will confess that I was not displeased by their interest once they demonstrated that they were not going to act on it right then and there."

"Good males don't do that, Laesa. No male has the right to force his attentions on you or make you do anything you don't want to. As far as I'm concerned any man who tries that kind of shit isn't worthy to breathe the same air as you. You're not on Tartarus anymore. Remember that."

"I wake up every day grateful that I am free now, but it's not easy to let go of the past," Laesa said.

Sophie surprised her by coming to her side and setting her hand on Laesa's shoulder.

"You'll find a way. You're stronger than you know. Look how much you've changed your life already and you only left Tartarus six months ago. You are finally becoming the person—uh, Tarin you were meant to be. You're an artist making a name for yourself. You've painted me a gorgeous mural that everyone admires, you have your paintings on display, and you're taking on clients. One of these days you're going to be famous, and I'll be able to tell everyone I knew you back before you were discovered."

Laesa leaned into her friend's gentle touch. "As always, you've been helpful and have given me some excellent advice. Tonight, I will think about all this. And I believe I will do some research on the Helios and their planet."

"Good. Now, eat the rest of your meal. I have a feeling you're going to need to keep your energy levels up. And since we're on the topic of energy levels, don't think that I don't know the real reason you're so tired lately. What you need to sustain yourself not even my fabulous lasagna can provide."

"You knew?" Laesa asked.

"Honey, you're Tarin, and you haven't kept company with a male since we've met. I'm betting you haven't dealt with that part of your nature in a while. Stars know I wouldn't either if I'd been through what you have. I don't know how long your people can go without feeding, but I'm betting you're pushing your limits."

Laesa nodded. "You would not be wrong in your assessment."

"I'll leave you to eat and think. Promise me you won't think too much." Sophie handed over the sketches and then departed with a friendly wave.

Laesa had only taken a few bites of her meal when her wrist unit chimed with an incoming message. She checked it with reluctance, well aware of who the sender likely would be. She skimmed the message and then deleted it without replying, exactly as she had with the dozens of messages that had come before.

Nevhar Antor was an old family friend. He'd helped her uncle find and retrieve her from the vile Lord who had enslaved her. Once she was free, Nevhar had wasted very little time making it known that he was interested in her.

In the months that she had stayed with her uncle while she had recovered, Nevhar had tried to convince her to agree to his offer. No matter how many times she declined, he had persisted. He had made it clear that he wanted to care for her and cherish her the way her father would have wanted, but to Laesa it had felt too much like trading one sort of slavery for another. Nevhar was of an age with her father and was a male of strong, traditional Tarin values. She knew she could never be happy with him.

Her uncle had hoped that she would agree to Nevhar's offer, but he didn't try to stop her once she made up her mind to leave Tartarus. He knew that she'd been scarred by grief and her captivity, and so he'd let her go, even providing her with a supply of credits to get her started in her new life.

That should have been the end of it, but Nevhar hadn't given up. Shortly after Sophie had given her the wrist unit, Laesa had arranged for a single message to be sent to her uncle. It hadn't been an easy task given that Tartarus was not as technologically advanced as the Alliance and their allies. She'd given him her new wrist unit's contact information in case of emergency. She had done it more as a gesture than anything else. She hadn't expected to ever hear from anyone on Tartarus again.

She'd been wrong. Nevhar had managed to convince her uncle to give him the contact information, and then he'd somehow managed to get a hold of a wrist unit. He must have gone to Hades Outpost, the only Alliance presence on Tartarus, to get one. It would have cost him dearly. Now, he sent her messages every week, always making the same offer. He wanted her for himself, and nothing she said seemed to deter him, so she'd taken to ignoring him instead.

After Nevhar's message, her mood didn't improve until she'd finished her meal and picked up her sketch-book again. As she filled the pages with countless images of the Torven brothers a smile stole over her lips, and she found herself looking forward to their next meeting.

There had been a time in her life that she'd done all she could to avoid attracting male attention out of fear of being singled out for her master's cruel attentions. That nightmare was over now, and she knew it was time to start living her life the way her parents would have wanted her to. The man who had terrorized her was dead by her uncle's hand. She had her freedom. It was time to reclaim what had been taken from her and enjoy herself again the way she had before she'd been enslaved.

Rhen arrived a few minutes early for his sitting with Laesa. He'd counted down the hours until his appointment, unable to focus on anything other than his desire to see her again. He and Sabar had spent their evening deep in conversation, and Laesa had been the only topic they'd discussed. She was an unexpected find, and they were both eager to spend time with her again. They'd done some cursory checking on her, only enough to confirm she was unattached. If she'd been spoken for, they'd have moved on. Since she appeared to be single, they had agreed they wanted to get to know her better.

She was Tarin, which meant she may not know that the Helios were a species who were influenced by their senses and instincts. They were both powerfully attracted to her on an almost primal level. That didn't mean she would automatically feel the same way about them. They were going to have to court her, and that was new territory for them. They were used to enjoying the company of the endless stream of females attracted to their wealth or looks. They were always brief affairs with no promises and no long-term expectations. Laesa was going to be a challenge. One they were both looking forward to.

Her spice and floral scent filled his lungs the moment he entered her cramped studio, and he took a slow, deep breath. Her scent was finer than the most expensive perfumes he'd ever known. He knew he'd never forget it as long as he lived.

"Hello and good day, Rhen Torven," Laesa said as she rose from her chair at the back of the room.

"And to you, Laesa. I hope you don't mind my being early. I was keen to get started."

"I was here early today as well," she confessed with a shy smile.

"Then let's begin. Where do you want me to sit?" he asked, doing his best to stay on point. She looked even lovelier than he remembered though there were faint shadows under her eyes that told him she hadn't slept any better than he had. He hoped that she'd been as lost in thoughts of them as they had been of her.

She beckoned him toward her. "Everything is arranged back here. Would you like something to drink before we begin? Once you're in position, it may be some time before you will be able to move again."

"I'm fine, thank you. I ate lunch with my brother before coming here. He sends his greetings, by the way, and wanted me to tell you he's looking forward to his sitting later this week." He moved to the back of the gallery and spotted a comfortable looking chair positioned across from a blank canvas.

"Tell him I look forward to that as well. Painting twins will be interesting. I want to capture your differences as well as your similarities. At least, I intend to try." She moved aside and gestured to the chair. "Please, sit."

"You think we have differences?" he asked as he settled into the chair.

"Of course," she replied.

"Tell me what you see. Everybody else has trouble telling us apart."

She laughed. "Which is why you wear your hair shorter than your brother, yes? To help identify yourself."

"The scars help, too. Though, not as much as you'd think." He touched the side of his head to indicate the strands of pure white hair that grew there.

"That is one way you differ from Sabar. It's not the only way. You are more controlled than he is. You move and speak different, as well."

Rhen was intrigued by her observations. "You saw a lot considering how little time we were here. You're right, I'm more restrained than my brother. At least I like to think so. I guess it's because I'm the older sibling, even if it's only by a matter of minutes."

She swallowed rapidly and lowered her gaze before speaking again. "I sometimes see things others miss because I am Tarin. We can sense energy in other beings. It lets me see my subjects in ways others cannot."

"That's an interesting talent to have." Rhen had heard about the Tarin ability but never given it much thought. He was looking forward to hearing more about her gift.

Laesa watched Rhen intently, looking for signs of unease at what she'd revealed. Not everyone reacted well to her explanation. Some feared she could read their thoughts and invade their privacy. Others found her ability strange and kept their distance from what they didn't understand. Rhen didn't show any such reaction. He seemed unperturbed by her explanation.

He was seated across from where she stood, looking entirely at ease. He'd dressed in a more casual style than he'd been yesterday. Instead of a tailored outfit, he'd chosen to wear a black shirt with loose sleeves and a V-neck he'd left only partially laced up. It suited him. He'd left his hair loose, and she was already considering what colors she would use to capture the red and gold shades.

"How does this work? What happens next?" he asked.

"Now, I tell you to get comfortable, and then I get you to move around until I think we've found the right pose. I like the way you're sitting right now. Relaxed, but in control." She hadn't meant to say that last bit out loud, but it was the truth. His confidence showed in the way he held himself, and she was undeniably attracted to him right now.

"Whatever you need me to do, Laesa."

He made the offer with the faintest hint of a wink, and her pulse sped up in response. "Do I have your permission to touch you? It will make it easier if I can guide you into the position I have in mind."

His smile deepened, and she caught a flicker of desire in his amber eyes. "You have my permission to touch me however you like."

Her entire body started to hum with arousal at his flirtatious comment, and she was momentarily grateful that his species weren't known to be telepathic. If they were, he'd know exactly how deeply his words were affecting her. She took his hands in hers, trying to keep her touch light but professional as she drew his arms into the right position. When she was satisfied, she stood up and took a few steps back to look at him again.

"Almost perfect," she said, pleased to note her voice was steady.

"Something still out of place?" he asked.

"Not at all. All that's missing is your smile. Unless you would rather look solemnly down upon anyone who views this painting?"

He grinned at her. "I don't think so. Dour looks of disapproval were never my favorite expressions. My mother will want to see us smiling."

"In that case, we're ready to begin. Now comes the boring part. I fear that you need to stay still. I'm going to capture a few images so that I can reference them later and then I'll start your portrait."

He started to nod, then stopped himself. "This is going to be harder than I thought."

Laesa hurried to take the images she needed, then took a seat in front of her easel. "We can talk as I work if you like. It should help pass the time."

"I'd like that," Rhen said. He wanted to speak with her. To know more about who she was, and how she'd wound up on an Alliance space station so far from Tartarus. He also wanted to pull her into his arms and kiss her senseless. It was likely a good thing he wasn't supposed to move. Otherwise, he'd be tempted to haul her into his lap. His skin still tingled where she'd touched him, and her scent was still wrapped around him like an invisible caress. The next few hours were going to be some of the longest of his life.

She gave him an assessing look, and her gaze never left him as she reached for a stylus of some sort and began moving it across the canvas in front of her. He couldn't see what she was drawing, and he found it fascinating that she could draw without really looking at what she was doing. Before he could comment on it, she began to speak.

"After we met yesterday, I realized I knew very little about your culture or world. My people have kept their distance from the other races. I've learned so much since I left Tartarus, but there's still much I don't know. I intended to do some general research on Helix, but I was distracted by the images I found of your world. It's beautiful, Rhen. So lush and vibrant. I think I would like to go there someday so I can experience it for myself."

Her expression was close to reverent as she spoke of his home, and he found himself making an unplanned offer. "If you ever decide to make the journey, Sabar and I would be happy to show you around our home world. We go back a few times a year to visit family and see to our business connections there. In fact, if you wanted to, you could travel with us on our ship, the *Auranox*."

"You'd take me to Helix?" she asked, her eyes wide and her expression a mix of disbelief and wariness.

"I wouldn't have offered if I didn't mean it. Yes, I'd take you home with me, Laesa. It would be my pleasure to show you the beauty of my home world. I understand that we don't know each other well enough for you to agree right now, but perhaps later you'll consider it."

"You really have your own ship? You can travel the stars at will?"

He nodded. "We have our own ship. Actually, we have several. In the beginning, we relied on others to transport our goods, but over time we've acquired a few freighters of our own. Their crews are loyal to us and very good at what they do."

"Thank you. That is a most generous offer. I'm not sure where I will go after I leave here. Perhaps I will get to see Helix sooner than I imagined I could," she said.

"As it happens, we're heading home once things are all arranged here. We travel a lot to keep an eye on our business, but we always know where we're going. How is it you don't know where you'll go next?"

Laesa shrugged. "I haven't been traveling for long. I booked passage to one of the Beta Stations because it was an easy journey. Once there, I met a human woman named Sophie and her bonded. She and I became friends. When her bonded were transferred to this station, she asked me to come here and paint a mural for her new restaurant. This is a military station, though. There isn't much demand for my work, so I'll need to move on eventually. I have been too busy to give much thought to where I'll go next. My life isn't very organized, yet. Not like you and your brother."

"We didn't start out organized. We left home not long after we returned from the Hunt. In the beginning, we had grand plans and not much else besides each other and a determination not to fail."

"If you will forgive my curiosity, what exactly is the Hunt?" she asked.

"It's a rite of passage for my race. The year we turn twenty we are sent deep into the jungle where things are still wild and dangerous. We have to make our own way out. Those who survive are marked with a scar over our hearts to signify we have proven our worth."

She stopped what she was doing and stared at him with wide eyes. "You said those who survive are marked. Not everyone lives?"

Rhen started to shake his head, then froze as he remembered he was supposed to stay still. "It would have no meaning if there was no risk involved."

"I am glad that you and your brother survived and proved your worth. Your parents must be proud of you. I cannot imagine how it would feel to have to watch those you love go and risk their lives that way. If you'll forgive me for asking, is that where you got your scars, during the Hunt?" She paused in her work to look at him, her lovely eyes filled with questions.

Rhen allowed himself a small smile. "I don't mind you asking. The scars are a memento of a reckless childhood. They're a reminder of what I managed to survive, despite my own stupidity. Sabar and I decided we knew better than our elders, and went too far into the jungle alone. We were attacked by a *bortax*. A nasty-tempered creature, and a fiercely territorial one. We killed it, but not before it clipped me with its claws. That was the last time I disobeyed the rules...for a few years, anyway. As for my parents, my fathers are very proud of us. My mother is, too, though she worries that we're going soft out here."

"Has she seen the two of you lately? I may not be an expert on the physiology of your race, but I can't imagine anyone describing you or your brother as *soft*."

"How would you describe us, then?" he asked, unable to resist the opening she'd given him.

"Powerful," she answered without hesitation. "You both look civilized on the surface, but I sense there's more to you than that. Yesterday you both showed hints of something else."

"Yesterday you caught us in an unguarded moment. We were…" He paused as he considered his next words. "We weren't expecting you."

"I wasn't expecting the two of you, either. I am glad you came to see my paintings. I will confess that I have been looking forward to speaking to you both again."

"It's the same for us. Would you consider letting us take you for dinner sometime? It would give us a chance to talk some more without you having to work at the same time."

Laesa nodded. Whatever was growing between the three of them, she wanted it to continue. Simply seeing Rhen again had her heart racing. The more they spoke, the more she discovered she enjoyed his company. If things went as well with Sabar, then she would be a fool to refuse their invitation. Sophie was right. It was time to move forward with her life.

"I would be pleased to share a meal with you and your brother," she said.

Rhen's eyes gleamed with satisfaction. "Good. I have the perfect place in mind already. Now, I think we have spoken enough about me. I want to hear about you, Laesa. Tell me something about yourself. Anything you like."

She took a moment to consider, then said, "Anything at all? Very well then. I've never seen an ocean except in pictures. I would like to see one someday. In fact, I have a list of places I'd like to visit, and things I'd like to see.

When my life was darkest, I'd escape by thinking about everything I hoped to see one day. I never truly thought I'd get a chance to experience any of them."

"And yet, here you are painting my portrait on an Alliance space station, lightyears away from your planet. Getting the chance to live our dreams seems to be something we have in common."

She liked that idea. "It would seem so."

"Tell me some of the other things that are on this list of yours."

She'd be more than happy to share some of the dreams that had kept her from losing all hope during her years as a slave, but there were some she wasn't ready to confess yet. Especially the one about wanting to see a Helios shift to their animal form. She had a feeling that if she did get to witness that, she'd want more than just to look. She'd want to touch, and that would lead down a path with only one outcome. Best not to mention it...yet.

The next few hours passed quickly as they talked and Laesa captured Rhen's likeness on her canvas. By the time they were done, her shoulders ached and her hands were tired. Even still, she was reluctant to end their session. Talking with Rhen had been fun and had given her a chance to get to know him. He was smart, with a quick wit, and an easy way about him she found as attractive as his handsome features and hard body.

Rhen got to his feet, rolling his shoulders several times to loosen them after so many hours of sitting still. "Do I get to see what you've got so far, or do I have to wait until it's done?" he asked.

"I would rather you not see it until it's finished. It doesn't look like much yet, and I want you to be happy that your credits were well spent." Laesa wiped the worst of the paint stains from her hands, and rose from her chair with a laugh and a smile.

"Okay. But you have to promise me that you won't let Sabar see his, either. And Laesa, I already know my credits were well spent. You don't have to worry about that."

She blushed. "Thank you. And you have my word that your brother will not see his before you do. You can both see them together once they're done. You were an excellent subject, by the way. You hardly moved at all."

"It was no hardship. I had your company to distract me. Now I'm free, though, I think I'm going to make use of the holo-room onboard our ship."

"That's a good idea. After I am finished here, I might take a walk around one of the viewing decks. I like looking out at the stars and the ships and wondering where they're from, and where they're going next. There's so much potential in this place. I like it. It makes me feel like anything is possible."

"I know what you mean," he said as he stared at her with eyes full of fire.

Before she knew what was happening, he was standing right beside her, stroking his thumb across her cheek.

"You've got a smudge of paint on your face. I thought I'd take care of it for you," he said by way of explanation.

"Uh, thank you," she said.

"You are very welcome. If you see the *Auranox* on your walk, you'd be welcome to come visit. If not, then I'll see you tomorrow for our next appointment. I enjoyed spending time with you today, lovely Laesa," he said, his voice dropping to a low murmur.

She gathered her courage and spoke. "I was about to go next door and have something to drink before I started painting again. Would you like to join me? I could show you the mural I created for my friend."

"There's nothing I would like more." He offered her his arm.

She only hesitated a moment before linking her arm with his. It was the first time since before she'd been enslaved that she had taken the initiative and asked a male to accompany her. It was a small step toward the future she'd once only dreamed of having.

CHAPTER THREE

Sabar caught several females watching him with interest as he made his way through the shopping level. Normally, he would have happily taken time out of his day to chat with a pretty woman, but not today. He hadn't so much as looked at another female since he'd met Laesa. She was far more interesting to him than anyone else had been in a long time.

He was impatient to get to know her better, and it rankled him that Rhen had spent hours with her over the last few days while he'd had to wait for his turn. Apart from a brief visit yesterday afternoon to say hello, he'd get his distance. He understood the logic. She needed time to get to know them without feeling overwhelmed, and they needed time to learn about her one on one. He just wasn't feeling overly patient at the moment.

The second he stepped into Laesa's small studio, he inhaled deeply, drinking in her scent. Lust rolled through him and he belatedly recalled his brother's warning that the sitting would be several kinds of torture. Clearly, he hadn't been kidding.

"It is a pleasure to see you, Sabar Torven," Laesa called out in welcome.

She was smiling as she came to meet him. She was wearing a dark dress of some kind, the skirt hiding her long legs save for a single, modest slit that ran up to her knee on one side. He couldn't see more than that because she had an apron on overtop, no doubt to prevent getting paint on her outfit.

"Hello, Laesa. How's your day gone? Well I hope."

"I have almost finished one of my commissions, and might have sold one of the landscapes, too. My day has gone very well, indeed."

"Don't sell all of them on us. My brother and I have been making inquiries. I expect to hear back from some of our art-loving clients in the next few days. It would be a sad day if you'd managed to sell out before they had a chance to see your work."

She shook her head and let loose a soft peal of laughter. "As if I could sell as many as that. There aren't that many art lovers on the whole station. Not to mention the fact my life is rather boring. I spend most of it creating new paintings, which means it would be nearly impossible for me to sell them all."

"If you love what you're doing with your life, then there's nothing boring about it. A great many people I know would love the chance to live their dreams and do what they're passionate about."

"You make it sound so glamorous."

He grinned. "That's my job description. Take the ordinary elements of life, and repackage them into something everyone wants to have. Then my brother and I sell it to them."

"I don't believe that to be true at all. The two of you must work very hard to have become as successful as you are. There's more to it than you're admitting to."

His heart warmed at her words. It wasn't often anyone acknowledged the work and sacrifice he and Rhen had done to get to where they were now. In part, it was his own fault. He'd deliberately cultivated a persona that was more playboy than businessman. He was the approachable twin, the one that would attend any function and spice up any gathering. Rhen played the role of serious partner, the steady, dependable, decision-maker. The truth was that they were both more than the roles they played. Not that many people ever looked beyond the surface. They saw what they wanted to see and nothing more. Laesa already saw more than many others ever had. It made her even more interesting to him.

"Are all artists as perceptive as you are?" he asked.

Laesa blushed slightly. "I don't know many artists, but I imagine they must be. If we weren't able to see things clearly, how would we be able to recreate it in our work?"

"I have to say I'm looking forward to seeing how you portray my brother and I. It isn't often I get to see through another's eyes."

Her face lit up with happiness. "That is exactly how I like to think of my portraits. I try to show people how others see them. I don't always succeed, but it's what I strive for. You will have to wait to see yours, though. I promised Rhen you wouldn't be allowed to peek since I did not permit him to."

"He mentioned that. He also said if I tried to convince you anyway, he'd kick my ass."

Laesa felt a pang of unease at the thought of the brothers fighting. "He wouldn't hurt you, would he?"

Sabar threw back his head and laughed. "Not even if he really tried to, which he wouldn't. We're too well matched for either of us to be able to beat up the other anymore. We sparred so much growing up we know all of the other one's moves."

"So you fight, but only to train? You wish to be ready to defend yourselves."

"We are Helios. We'd fight to the death to protect what is ours."

Sabar's words were roughened by a hint of a growl that had her taking a step backward.

Immediately he reached for her, regret flashing in his golden eyes. "You have nothing to fear from me, blossom. I would never hurt you."

"Not even if you were not exactly yourself at the time?" she asked, holding still as he took her hand in his.

For a moment, he looked puzzled. "Not myself? You mean...ah. You're talking about my ability to shapeshift. The beast I become is still me, Laesa. My mind in a different body, that's all. I'd not harm you in either form, and neither would Rhen."

"I'm sorry if I gave insult. It's just that you growled, and that is a sound I have learned heralds anger and...

repercussions," she said, her gaze dropping to the floor as she uttered the last word.

Sabar's eyes darkened. "One day, I hope you'll tell me what happened that put the shadow of fear in your beautiful eyes."

"One day, I'll tell you, though if you know anything about some of my people's darker traditions, I think you can guess."

He growled again, but this time, she could sense by his energy that his anger was not directed at her.

"You'll never have to fear either of us, Laesa. If you ever wish to seek revenge on the ones who harmed you, just give us their names and we'll see it done."

"There is no one left to seek revenge on. My uncle saw to that when he tracked me down and freed me." Her uncle's greatest regret was that it had taken him so long to find her. In the beginning everyone believed she had died with her parents. Once he learned that wasn't the case, he hadn't rested until she was safe. He was her uncle, though. He'd protected her because that was what family did for each other. It was strangely pleasing to her to know Sabar would do that for her despite the fact they had only just met.

He still had hold of her hand, his fingers caressing her palm. "I'd do whatever it took to banish those shadows from your eyes forever."

"Why?" she asked. "We only met a few days ago."

Sabar's lips curled into a slow, sensual smile. "Have dinner with us tomorrow night and you can ask me that question again. I promise I'll answer you then."

"Tomorrow night, then. I look forward to it."

Laesa's hand was trembling as she withdrew it from his. There was no denying her attraction to the two brothers. They made her heart race and her blood burn in a way she hadn't felt since before she'd been enslaved. Whatever was forming between them, she wanted to pursue it wherever it may lead.

Sabar's second sitting was going well. In fact, Laesa had enjoyed every second of her time with both brothers over the last four days. They had been interesting subjects to paint, and she'd gotten to know them both in the hours they'd spent together.

Things had gone so well, that the greatest challenge she'd had was finding the right pose for Sabar. No matter how he sat, he always appeared to be on the verge of moving. Eventually, she'd simply painted him standing up. He was currently leaning up against the far wall in a casual stance that suited his personality and appearance. He'd chosen to wear dark brown leather pants that fitted him perfectly, along with a simple white shirt beneath a leather vest. The outfit was well made and clearly expensive, but it also reminded her of what she'd read about the Helios. They appeared civilized, but beneath the veneer, they were still a wild and fearsome species. She suspected Sabar had chosen his clothing for precisely that reason. It was something she intended to ask him about when they knew each other better.

They had talked for all of yesterday's session as well as this one. He'd told her stories about growing up on Helix, making her laugh often as he described the trouble he and Rhen had gotten into. She'd shared a few stories about Tartarus, but mostly she'd spoken about her new life as an artist. He had been keenly interested to hear her impressions of everything she'd experienced, from the transports she'd taken to the food being served at Asylum, the Krytos sanctuary on the station.

She was nearly finished with the day's work when her wrist unit chimed, indicating she had a new message. Likely, it was Sophie checking in on things. Laesa set down her brush. "I think this is a good time to stop. You must be tired of standing there by now."

Sabar straightened up and reached up to rub the back of his neck. "Until we started this project, I had no idea standing still would be that difficult."

"Everyone thinks it will be easy until they have to do it. Go and stretch your legs, if you like. I will clean up here and then prepare to close up for the night."

He nodded and moved away from the wall. "Is there anything I can do to help?"

"If you could bring in the one painting that's on an easel near the entrance, I would appreciate it. I will not be long."

"Take your time. You've been sitting there working for hours. We're in no hurry."

"You don't mind waiting?" she asked.

He shrugged. "Why would I mind? My time isn't any more valuable than yours."

Laesa knew that wasn't true. She was a simple artist while Sabar was a successful merchant. His time was worth far more than hers would ever be. She appreciated his words, though. It had been a long time since she'd felt truly valued by a male. Both Sabar and Rhen had given her that gift. They made her feel special. In fact, in the days since she'd first found them in her shop, they had treated her so well that she felt as if they had known each other far longer than they really had.

She checked her messages and laughed when she saw that it was indeed Sophie asking how things were progressing. She sent her a quick note saying all was well, and looked up to find Sabar watching her.

"You're smiling. Good news?" he asked.

"Not good news, a good friend checking up on me. When I leave here, I'm going to miss her. Sophie has been very supportive and helpful. She's the reason I came to the station in the first place. She encouraged me to display my work, and showed me that I can be successful."

"Sounds like the best sort of friend you can have. I want you to know that Rhen and I want you to succeed, and not only because we're hoping to help sell your paintings and make a profit for all of us. You have a real talent, and I want others to see what you can do."

"Thank you. It…it means a great deal to me that you would say that."

Before she could do more than blink, Sabar was standing in front of her. "I'm not merely saying it. I meant every word."

"I know you do. That's why it means so much." She reached out and brushed her fingers over the back of his hand. "You make me feel special."

He twisted his hand and captured her fingers in his. "You are special, blossom. Don't you ever doubt it."

"Why do you call me blossom?" she asked, her heart beating a wild dance in her chest at his touch.

"Your scent reminds me of the night flowers that grow back home. They're beautiful, but so delicate they hide from the harsh heat of the day and only bloom in the moonlight."

"They sound lovely."

"They are, and so are you." Sabar moved in close enough that she could feel the heat of his body. He brushed his mouth against hers, and murmured her name before retreating again.

"Sabar, did you just kiss me?" she whispered.

"I did. And unless you slap me and tell me to never do that again, I plan on kissing you as often as I can." He winked at her and lifted her hand to his mouth to kiss her fingertips before releasing her hand.

"I have no intention of telling you to cease, and I am certainly not going to slap you. But I think you knew that already."

"I hoped, but it's a female's right to choose. Remember that. Whatever happens between the three of us, it's your decision."

Sabar wanted nothing more than to haul Laesa into his arms and kiss her until neither of them could think. Being in her company for the last two days had been a sweet torment. Her soft-spoken demeanor hid a quick and agile mind. She was their match in so many ways, and he was starting to hope that one day they would claim her as their own. First, though, they needed to explain to her what they hoped to have with her and what it would mean to be their companion. She wasn't from their culture, and they couldn't make any assumptions about what she knew about the Helios. Information on Tarins wasn't easy to come by, either. They would have to figure this out as they went along.

He wanted to know about her life back on Tartarus. If she'd been abused the way he suspected, then they would find a way to give her all the understanding she needed to heal from what she endured. More than that, he wanted to protect her from every experiencing that kind of pain again.

"My decision. I will remember that. Will you give me a few minutes to finish here and tidy myself up for dinner?" She smiled at him, and her beautiful obsidian eyes shone with new confidence.

He nodded. "I'll be waiting outside. Join me when you're ready, but don't rush on my account. This night is all about you, Laesa."

"I will see you out front in a little while."

Sabar wandered to the front of the gallery and claimed a portion of wall outside. The air out here was heavy with the delicious odor of roasted meat and other dishes, and he tracked the scents to the restaurant next door. This would be Sophie's Café, the place that Laesa's human friend owned. Rhen had mentioned eating there the other day. As if his thoughts had summoned her, a petite, blonde human female appeared at the door and smiled up at him as if she knew him.

"Hi again. Oh, wait, no. You're not the one I met. You must be the other brother. Sabar, right?"

"I'm Sabar. And you must be Sophie. It's nice to meet you."

"Where's Laesa?" Sophie asked, glancing around.

"She's finishing up inside and then freshening up before I take her to dinner. She'll be along shortly."

The tiny human looked up at Sabar with fire in her eyes. "In that case, I've got something I need to say to you. I expect you and your brother to take good care of my friend, cat boy. She's special, and she deserves nothing but happiness after all the shit she's survived already."

Cat boy? Sabar grinned down at the feisty female with amusement. "You have my word she will be treated with all the respect and care she deserves, and more. If I have my way, she will never suffer another day of unhappiness in her life."

Sophie's expression softened. "I'm glad to hear it. Sorry for the show of force, but I worry about her."

"No offense taken. You're her friend, and you want to protect her. So do I."

"I only know a little of what happened to her before she got here, but it's enough to make me grateful I wasn't born a Tarin female. Being an infertile female back on Earth had its rough patches, but meeting Laesa made me realize I had it comparatively easy."

Sabar growled low in his throat. "No female should ever have to live through what Laesa experienced."

"Good answer. You and your brother might be exactly what Laesa needs in her life," Sophie said with an approving grin.

"I sincerely hope so. I'm starting to suspect that she is what's missing in ours."

The human female's eyes went wide with surprise at his statement. "What—"

The rest of her query went unspoken as Laesa joined them. "Good evening, Sophie. Have you been making Sabar's acquaintance while I was getting ready?"

"I was, and now I'm going to make myself scarce. You look gorgeous, Laesa. Have fun, and don't do anything I wouldn't do!" With that, Sophie waved to them both and vanished back into her restaurant.

Laesa hadn't been gone long, but she'd managed to transform herself while she was out of his sight. The shape-concealing apron she'd been wearing all day was gone, revealing the sapphire-blue wrap dress she'd had on beneath. The soft fabric clung to her curves, showing off a figure that had been hidden until this moment.

Holy fuck, she was stunning.

"I wasn't certain what would be appropriate to wear to dinner since I didn't know where we were going. Will this suffice?" she asked, skimming her hand over the dress.

"You look perfect. As for where we're going, Rhen and I have arranged for a special meal to be prepared and served onboard our ship."

Laesa's heart skipped a beat. "Dinner is on the *Auranox*? Just the three of us?"

Sabar nodded. "You, me, and Rhen. We gave the rest of the staff and crew the night off."

"You have staff?" she asked.

"We do. A flight crew as well as a few others. Jonah is a talented chef who travels with us. Ashar acts as our personal assistant. He's the most organized and patient being I've ever met. Eventually, you'll meet them all, but we wanted to keep you to ourselves for a while longer."

"And dinner is on the ship. You really do want me all to yourselves." The idea of being alone with the two of them had her body aching with need. She wanted to be with them. To talk, and laugh, and be in their company. Every night she'd thought about the time she'd spent with each of them with happiness and anticipation of seeing them again.

Now, she yearned for more than their companionship. She trusted them. Desired them. She suspected that if she went with them tonight, she could have everything she wanted. Her people were sexual by their very nature. She'd denied that part of herself because she needed to feel in control of her life. Before she'd been taken, she'd enjoyed the company of males, feeding when she needed to without hesitation.

Her time as a slave had made her wary, but she didn't feel that way with Rhen and Sabar. When Sabar had told her that whatever happened, it would be her choice, she'd finally felt ready to take the next step.

"We do want you. We wanted the three of us to be able to be alone with no interruptions. We're possessive males, blossom. When we see something we like, we go after it, and once we have it, we don't let go." Sabar winked at her and then took her hand in his.

She glanced down at their joined hands. "That would explain how the two of you have done so well for yourselves. Does this mean you aren't going to be letting go of my hand?"

"Not until I have to. I assume you'll need both hands to eat, though, so I planned on releasing you once we get onboard."

She laughed. "Very well. Take me to your ship, Sabar, and on the way you can tell me what it's like to live on a starship."

He started walking toward the docking ring. "It's amazing most of the time, though it can feel a little cramped when we've been together too long. Living onboard also means we have room and privacy to shift when we need to. Plus, we already have everything we could want set up onboard, including a holo-room. You'll see what I mean when we get there."

"If I had a holo-room of my own, I'd never leave. I'd spend my days exploring programs of every world I could find, and painting what I saw."

"You're welcome to use ours, you know. But you'd have to leave it sometimes. That's where we go to shift. For some strange reason, the other races tend to get agitated if they see an eight-hundred-pound carnivore with big teeth and claws running loose. Not to mention the fact the Alliance gets their uniforms in a twist if we shift while on one of their stations."

Laesa struggled to imagine the male walking with her transformed into the creature he'd described. "Eight-hundred pounds? I didn't realize your other form was so big!"

"When you're ready, we'll show you that part of ourselves, but there's no rush. We're still getting to know each other," Sabar said.

He led her to the far side of X21, to one of the station's docking bays, then to where their ship was berthed. As they approached, the door to their berth slid open and Rhen stepped out to greet them. He was dressed in a similar fashion to Sabar, only his leathers were pure black instead of brown.

"Hello again, Laesa. I'm glad you're here." Rhen bowed slightly as he greeted her.

"Hello and good eve to you, Rhen. I am pleased to be here."

Rhen took her free hand in his and started to draw her inside, only to stop when she laughed.

"Is there something wrong?" he asked.

She glanced at the hand he was holding and then to the one Sabar still had hold of. "Your brother mentioned to me on the way here that once you two have hold of something you want, you don't tend to let go. I'm starting to see what he meant."

Rhen's mouth quirked up into a lopsided grin that made him look far less serious than his usual demeanor. "Guilty as charged. I can't wait to hear what other tidbits my brother shared. If he told you anything about me, please assume it was all lies. I'm the good twin."

"Like hell you're the good one. Don't you listen to him, blossom. He's delusional."

"I happen to think you're both good. If I didn't, I wouldn't be here," Laesa declared. It was the truth, too. In her heart, she knew they would never hurt her. She'd spent hours in their company now, and in all that time she'd read enough of their energies to know that they were good, honorable males.

"You have no idea how happy I am you're here. Come inside, Laesa. Let us show you our home."

Rhen had been prepared for his body's reaction to Laesa's scent, but it still affected him like a punch to the gut. To know that she was here in their home at last had him instantly hard and aching. He'd taken her hand because the need to touch her had been overwhelming, and holding her hand was a safer move than giving in to his need to have her in his arms so he could kiss her until they were both breathless.

She let him guide her inside, and her mouth formed a perfect "o" of surprise as she got her first look at their ship. The *Auranox* had once been a freighter. From the outside, it still looked like one, but the interior had been completely redesigned. They'd replaced the standard layout with more spacious rooms, wider corridors, and a carefully crafted balance of technology and elegance. The cargo bays were now living quarters and offices, allowing for far more living space than was usual. It allowed them to travel and do business in comfort anywhere in the cosmos.

"This is not what I expected when I heard you lived aboard a ship. This is luxurious compared to the transports I traveled on to get here."

Sabar chuckled. "You haven't seen the good parts yet. Later on, we'll take you on a tour. You ready for dinner?"

"I am. In fact, I'm quite hungry. I was so busy today, I forgot to stop and eat lunch."

"You should have said something. Come on, dinner is this way," Sabar said, squeezing her hand and drawing her down the main corridor until he reached the holo-room. He tapped the activation code into the console and within seconds the door slid open, revealing the first of the surprises they'd organized for Laesa.

She stepped into the room and gasped. "Is this—is this Helix?"

Laesa hadn't spent much time in holo-rooms, but she knew that was what she was standing in. There was no other way to explain how she'd suddenly found herself surrounded by warm air and lush vegetation. The three of them stood on a hilltop with an unfamiliar sky overhead. She was tempted to kick off her shoes to walk across the small meadow of thick, blue-green grass and wildflowers laid out like a fragrant carpet beneath her feet. Beyond the hilltop, they were surrounded by heavy jungle that spread out in all directions as far as she could see. When she breathed in, the scent of sun-warmed soil blended with the lighter notes of flowers and green, growing things.

It was beautiful.

Rhen nodded. "This is Helix. At least, it's as close to it as we can get without going home. When you mentioned you'd like to see our home world one day, I knew it would be the perfect setting for dinner."

The breeze shifted, bringing with it the tantalizing scent of food. Off to the side was a wooden table laden with a number of covered dishes and set with three place settings.

"It is the most beautiful setting for a meal I've ever seen."

Sabar released her hand at last. He walked over to the table and pulled out a chair for her. "The setting is nice, but I've only got eyes for you, blossom."

"For once, I agree with my brother. You're far more beautiful than the view." Rhen escorted her to the table, pressing a kiss to the palm of her hand before letting go of her.

Laesa sat down and looked at the feast before her, then at the two males taking their seats on either side of her. They'd done this all for her. The thought that they cared enough to set all this up made her even more certain of her plans. This was what she wanted. *They* were what she wanted. Rhen and Sabar were handsome and charming, but more than that, they treated her like she mattered. They looked at her like she was a treasure to be cherished instead of a tool to be used and cast aside.

She'd found the ones she wanted to be with. It was time to take the next step in reclaiming her life, and let the scars of her past finally finish healing.

CHAPTER FOUR

Sabar ate without tasting anything that passed his lips. The wine could have been water for all the effect it had on him. Laesa had all his attention. He watched, fascinated as she slowly bloomed over the course of the meal. They'd been right to have dinner here, away from everyone and free from interruptions. She was at ease this way, and by the time they finished their meal, she was laughing and aglow with enjoyment.

She was also utterly breathtaking.

"Computer, initiate sunset program."

Rhen's command signaled the next phase of the evening had started, and Sabar pushed back from the table. He turned to watch as a large, single-seat swing materialized on the far side of the clearing. The swing was a replica of the one that sat in their parents' backyard on Helix, right down to the red and yellow stripes on the thick, comfortable cushions that covered the wooden frame. It was positioned to face the setting sun as it dropped below the soft, rolling hills that marked the distant horizon.

"Join us, Laesa? We can watch the sunset in comfort, and shortly after that, the moons will rise. I have to admit that this is one of the things I miss when we're in space. No suns or moons to watch as they rise and set."

Laesa nodded and stood. "I would love to sit and watch the sunset with the two of you. I never even thought about such things until I had left Tartarus behind. I miss the little things that come from being on a planet. Things like sunsets, and thunderstorms, and the sound of the wind blowing through the trees outside my window."

"Like I said, blossom. You can come here and use this room anytime you like." Sabar rose a split-second before his brother and took Laesa's hand. He led her to the swing, helping her to get seated while Rhen held it steady.

"If there's anything you desire, anything at all, you only have to ask," Rhen added as he joined them.

They sat on either side of her, Sabar draping a possessive arm around her shoulders, while Rhen took her hand and threaded their fingers together before setting their joined hands on his thigh. The sunset was painting the sky with colors so beautiful it made her artist's soul sing but she couldn't keep her attention on it. Not when she had Rhen and Sabar sitting so close. Hard, muscular thighs pressed against hers, and she could feel their body heat warming her skin.

"The other day, I asked Sabar a question. He told me to ask him again tonight. I think now would be the right time to ask it. We haven't known each other very long, so why is my happiness important to the two of you?"

Sabar leaned in and brushed a soft kiss to her forehead. "Because there's something very special about you. You bring out the best in us."

Rhen chuckled. "Poetic, but not very clarifying for our female. Laesa, our species are strongly affected by scents. The moment we walked into your shop, your scent called to me. To both of us. That kind of attraction doesn't happen very often. It made us want to spend time with you and get to know you better.

Laesa blinked several times as she tried to grasp what they were telling her. "You want me because I smell good?"

Sabar snorted with laughter. "Nice work, Rhen. I think you managed to confuse her even more. What we're trying to say is that we care about you, Laesa. We're attracted to you, yes. But now, it's become something more than physical attraction. What we want it isn't a fling. At least, that's not what we're hoping for. You're beautiful, talented, and smart. I can see you being part of our lives for a long time to come."

"Are you telling me that you would consider being my consorts? Both of you?" she asked, using the Tarin term for a permanent partner. Her emotions were spinning out of control, and she felt as if the only thing keeping her grounded was their touch.

Rhen nodded. "Eventually, yes. If you decide that's what you want, too."

"We want you, Laesa," Sabar said.

"It's my choice, though, right? I really should have read up on your species like I had planned. I'm going to have questions about all this."

"Ask anything you like. To be honest, we've got a few questions of our own. Your world has been closed off for so long there isn't a lot of information about your species, and most of what there is only refers to the males," Sabar said.

She laughed a little. "I can imagine what one of your questions will be, so I might as well answer it. Yes, I feed the same way as the males of my species."

"Holy stars above," Rhen muttered.

"And if you had a companion—what you'd call a consort, then you only feed from them?" Sabar asked.

"If I were to be blessed with a consort of my own, then they would be the only one I ever fed from. Once we bonded, he...or they, would be all I ever needed."

Sabar uttered a low rumble that sounded remarkably similar to the low purring noise Sophie's pet feline, Snuggles, made when he was happy.

"I want to be that for you," Sabar said, drawing her in close.

His lips claimed hers in a heated kiss that said more than words ever could. His mouth slanted across hers, his hand leaving her shoulder to cradle the back of her head as he took the kiss deeper. His tongue traced the seam of her lips, and she parted them, allowing him entrance. Rhen lifted her hand from his lap and raised it to his lips, nibbling on her fingers and sucking the tips into the heat of his mouth.

Need filled her, slickening her pussy and making her clit throb in time to her rapidly beating heart. It was difficult to think past the demands of her body, but she clung to the last frayed edges of her control. There was one more thing she needed to know before she let go. She pulled back from Sabar just enough to be able to speak.

"I was a slave once already. That life is behind me now, and I've been free for almost a year. Before we go any further, I have to know. If I'm with you two, will you let me have a life of my own? Will I still be free?" she asked.

Both men went still and quiet.

Rhen's stomach twisted at the thought of what Laesa must have endured to even ask that question. He rose from the swing, then crouched on the ground at Laesa's feet. The next words he spoke coming straight from his heart. "You have my word as a Helios warrior that as long as you are with us, no matter how that relationship is defined, you'll never be treated as a slave. You'll be an equal partner in all aspects of our lives."

"You have my word as well. I already told you, blossom. The choice lies with you. It always will," Sabar said.

"And we don't have to rush this. We have time. All the time you need. We won't claim you until we're all sure this is what we want," Rhen added.

"I hope it doesn't take you too long to decide, though. I'm not a patient male. I'd be lying if I said that I didn't want to see my mark on your skin. I want the world to know you belong to us," Sabar said.

Laesa smiled and nodded. "You did warn me you would be possessive. These marks you speak of, they would also make it clear that the two of you belong to me?"

"They would."

"Then I will keep that in mind. I've seen the way other females watch the two of you. I don't like it."

Rhen rose up until he was eye-to-eye with his beautiful Tarin. As he leaned in to kiss her, he made another vow. "If you want me, Laesa, then I'm all yours. From now until my ancestors call me home."

She was smiling as his lips touched hers.

He kissed her slowly, savoring every moment. She tasted of wine and the glazed fruit tart she'd eaten for dessert. Her lips were soft and warm against his, and when she moaned into his mouth, it was the sweetest sound he'd ever heard.

"Will you stay with us tonight, blossom?" Sabar asked.

"Yes."

That single syllable, uttered in barely more than a whisper, was enough to set Rhen's world afire.

"Say that again," Rhen said, staring into her dark eyes.

She laughed, a joyful sound that filled the clearing with its music. "Yes. Yes, I'll stay with you both this eve. And you should know I have been injected with something that will prevent me from conceiving."

He kissed her again. Their tongues danced, lips mated, the scent of her filling his senses until he was nearly drunk with it. Soft fingers slipped beneath his shirt to stroke the bare skin of his chest. Her touch was like a blazing torch, sending sparks of heat sizzling across his flesh. Sabar rose from his seat on the swing and vanished from view, only to reappear behind Laesa.

Rhen moved back as his brother leaned down and nuzzled the side of Laesa's neck. One day soon, he hoped that she'd allow them to bite her there, leaving their marks on her forever. He could already imagine the tiny, starburst-shaped scars on her skin and the thought made his cock throb behind the confines of his pants.

Laesa was relishing every second with the men she'd chosen to take as her lovers. Sabar's mouth was on her throat, and Rhen's hands were on her thighs. The fabric of her skirt was pushed up, baring her legs. Sabar's hands cupped her breasts as Rhen dipped his head to blaze a trail of open-mouthed kisses to her inner thigh. The wrap-around dress that had fit perfectly only a moment ago now felt two sizes too small. She reached over and tugged at the ties that held the fabric in place.

As the dress came undone, she shrugged out of it and let it fall away. Both men groaned in unison as she bared herself to their gazes.

"You're so damned beautiful," one of them muttered and for the life of her, she couldn't tell which one had spoken.

She turned her head and kissed Sabar as his hands found her breasts again. Strong fingers tweaked and toyed with her nipples until they were so sensitive that every touch sent jolts of pleasure straight to her clit. Rhen's hands were on her thighs, pushing them wider as he worked his way up ever closer to her pussy. She tangled her hands in Rhen's hair, pulling him closer to where she needed him to be. He was chuckling at her eagerness as he parted her folds with his fingers and ran the tip of his tongue in a slow, lazy circle around her clitoris.

"Please!" she said, her cry caught in the heated depths of Sabar's mouth.

Instead of continuing, Rhen moved back and blew a puff of air across her folds. "Patience, love. We have all night."

"No. Please. I...I need this. I haven't fed in so long. I need you both, now."

"You should have told us." Sabar broke their kiss to speak to her.

"I'm telling you now," she replied.

"We'll have this conversation later," Rhen said, working his fingers into her pussy. He slid one finger into her slick channel, testing her readiness. When he added a second finger, she trembled, and when he began fucking her with strong, steady strokes, she arched her hips off the swing to meet each thrust.

Sabar brushed one last kiss to her mouth before moving back from the swing. Rhen's fingers were moving faster, distracting her from everything else. She was nearly mindless with the need to come by the time Sabar reappeared. He was naked as he sat down beside her. His golden skin painted by the fading light of the setting sun, and his amber eyes were bright with desire as he turned to stare at her.

"Come here," he said, patting his chest.

Beneath his hand was a small scar, and she moved closer to look at it. "Is this the scar you received for surviving the Hunt?"

"Yes." Before she knew what was happening, he and Rhen had lifted her up and settled her so that she was facing Sabar, her thighs straddling his lap. Sabar's hands stayed on her hips as she explored his naked body. He was built like a warrior should be. Big, with corded muscles moving underneath his golden skin. His cock was wedged between her thighs, thick and hard as iron. He kissed her and then shifted his body lower so that his cock was pressing against her entrance, and his head was level with her breasts. His lips found her breast and drew one taut nipple into his mouth, teasing her.

Rhen re-appeared behind the swing. He leaned past his brother to nuzzle at her ear and whisper, "Ride him. Take what you need."

Her hand trembled as she reached between her thighs and wrapped her fingers around Sabar's shaft. She moved slowly, caught between the demands of her body and painful memories of the countless times she'd done this because she'd had no other choice.

As if sensing her conflict, Sabar lifted a hand to cup her cheek and gave her a slow wink before lifting his mouth from her flesh to speak. "Your choice, remember?"

Her choice. That's what they'd both promised her. Tonight nothing would happen unless she wanted it to. It was the reminder she needed to be able to banish her dark thoughts.

"I choose to be with you," she whispered as she rolled her hips and took him into her body. She set her hands on the back of the swing to help her keep her balance as Sabar raised himself up and drove his cock deep inside.

"Laesa!" Sabar cried out her name as they became one.

She stared into his eyes, falling into their golden depths. She opened a link between them, letting his energy flow into her. It was primal and pure, and like nothing she'd ever experienced before. She threw back her head and gave in to her instincts, savoring his essence as she rode him hard.

Sabar was almost out of his mind with pleasure. She was finally naked and in his arms. He wanted to lick every inch of her body and cover her in his scent. For the first time in his life, he wanted to sink his teeth into a female and mark her as his own. Buried balls-deep inside her was where he'd dreamed of being from the moment he'd first caught her scent. Now that the moment was here, it was more than he'd imagined it could be.

Unable to hold back, he gripped her hips and lifted her a few inches higher. The added space gave him room enough to thrust harder and faster. Soon what little control he had left began to shred, and the world shrank down to a handful of details. The heat of her tight little pussy. The pulse and flutter of her inner walls gripping his dick. The sweet sound of her breathless moans as she met him thrust for thrust.

She came with a wild cry. Head thrown back, eyes closed, her beautiful face flushed as she was carried away by her pleasure. Watching her come was enough to trigger his own orgasm. It hit with the force of a meteor strike and sent him spinning out of control. He emptied himself inside of her, and once again, he had to fight the urge to sink his fangs into her throat and mark her as his.

"You are the most glorious, sexy, incredible female in the cosmos. In case there was any doubt in your mind, we are never, ever letting you go, Laesa," Sabar said once he had breath in his lungs to speak again.

Her eyes fluttered open and she gave him a smile so sweet it made his heart sing. "I have no desire to let go of you, either. Never in my life have I felt anything like that."

Laesa lifted her arms over her head and stretched. She was already feeling stronger, not just physically but emotionally, too. The scars of the past would always be with her but now she knew they wouldn't rule her. She was truly free.

"How are you feeling?" Rhen asked. He'd moved again and was standing only a few feet away. His chest was bare, as were his feet, but his pants were still on, and he looked at her with a trace of concern in his eyes.

"Wonderful. I haven't felt like this in…" She paused for a moment. "I do not believe I have ever felt like this before."

"Are you ready for more, then?" he asked, holding out his hand to her.

"Yes, please." She kissed Sabar one last time before leaving his arms and rising from the swing. The sunset was nearly over, and the sky overhead was a deep, twilight purple already dusted with stars.

"Then come to me, love," Rhen said, still holding out his hand in invitation.

The worry was gone from his expression, replaced by need. She kicked off her shoes and walked across the soft grass to take his hand, letting him draw her in tight to his body. He slid his fingers into her hair and kissed her hungrily, holding her close as his mouth plundered hers.

She slid her hands up his well-muscled body, exploring every line and sinew along the way. Just as her hands reached the tops of his shoulders, he broke their kiss and lifted his head. "Hold on to me. I think it's time we moved to the bedroom."

"Guest suite or one of ours?" Sabar asked.

"Guest suite's bed's not big enough for all three of us. We'll go to mine. That way we can sleep comfortably."

"Sleep? You wish me to sleep with you tonight?" Laesa asked, surprised.

"Fuck yes, we want you to sleep with us," Sabar said from somewhere behind her.

"Of course we do. I'm a greedy male. Now I have you naked, I intend to keep you like this as long as I can. I want to hold you as you sleep, and be there when you wake up," Rhen told her.

Joy filled her heart and tears stung her eyes at their words. "I would like that very much."

"Good. Then put your arms around my neck. We'll come back to watch the rest of this program another day."

Rhen wanted the female in his arms more than he wanted his next breath, but he knew his needs had to come second to Laesa's. She had to understand what they wanted was so much more than sex, and it would take time to prove to her that she wasn't a plaything or a passing fancy. He lifted her into his arms and carried her out of the holo-room with Sabar only a few steps behind them.

It was a short walk to his bedroom, but tonight, it felt far longer than ever before. No doubt because every step brought him closer to finally getting what he craved most. Her.

His bedroom door slid open with a wave of his hand, and he stepped inside. It wasn't until the door closed behind the three of them that Rhen felt the full weight of what they were doing. By unspoken agreement, he and Sabar never brought their lovers to the ship. Laesa was the first one. If the gods were kind, she'd also be the last.

Laesa lifted her head from Rhen's shoulder as they entered his room. She was curious to see what his personal space looked like. As the lights came on, she found herself surrounded by solid wooden furnishings and thick rugs woven into elaborate and colorful designs. That's all she had time to register before she found herself placed in the center of a large bed. She expected Rhen to join her there, but when she looked up, he hadn't moved. Instead, he was staring at her, his hands on the fly of his pants, and his eyes full of primal need.

"Perfect," he murmured.

"Hardly," she protested.

"Absolutely," was all he said as he stripped off the last of his clothing.

He was the mirror image of his brother in every way. A gorgeous male in his prime. "I think you're the perfect one. You and Sabar—one day I'm going to sketch you both in the nude."

Rhen was laughing as he joined her on the bed. "You can draw us any way you like, but I have to warn you that if you have us naked, we're not going to be able to hold still for hours. That was hard enough to do fully clothed."

She tangled her fingers in his hair and grinned at him. "I promise we'll take breaks. Seeing you naked might be something of a temptation for me as well."

His big body moved over hers, pinning her gently to the mattress. He braced his upper half a few inches above hers, his head lowered to brush tender kisses to her mouth and cheeks.

"Now we do this my way," he murmured.

Before she could ask what he meant, he showed her. He started moving down her body, drifting feather soft kisses across her skin as he made his way lower. When he reached her breasts, he drew circles around her nipples with the tip of his tongue, alternating from one to the other until she thought she'd lose her mind.

"Rhen, please. More. I need more than this."

"How much more, blossom? Do you want me to join you?" Sabar asked from his vantage point across the room.

"I—I don't know. Rhen?" she looked to Rhen for guidance, but he only smiled and shook his head.

"It's your choice, Laesa," he said.

Holy hellfire.

She hesitated, but only for a moment. It was her choice, but the truth was there was no decision to make. She wanted them both. "Come here, Sabar."

"Good choice," Rhen said before kissing his way down her body again.

He'd barely reached her navel by the time Sabar was settled on her other side, then she was caught up in a whirlwind of pleasure and sensation. Four hands caressed her. Two mouths tasted and teased. Sabar focused on her breasts while Rhen moved ever lower until his tongue was stroking along the seam of her pussy. He parted her folds with his fingers, exposing her clit to his questing tongue and she moaned as he sucked the delicate bundle of nerves into his mouth.

She'd never been seduced like this. Not before she'd been enslaved, and certainly not afterward. She rode each cresting wave of pleasure as it washed through her, each one coming harder and faster than the last. She felt as though she were being bathed in flames. Every kiss and caress built on the one before until she was trembling with raw need.

Every stroke of Rhen's tongue and nip of Sabar's fangs pushed her closer to the brink. When Rhen slid a finger into her tight channel, it only took a few pumps of his hand to send her hurtling over the edge.

"I'm never going to get tired of watching you do that," Sabar whispered as he moved back from her, giving his brother space enough for him to claim a place above her.

"Me either." Rhen settled himself into the cradle of her thighs and sealed her mouth with a sizzling kiss that promised more passion to come.

His cock pressed against her entrance and then slid inside, filling her inch by inch. She opened herself to his energy and let it pour into her. He was inside her now in more ways than one, a possession that went beyond the physical.

The three of them were connected now, and in her heart, she knew this was only the beginning.

Rhen didn't let himself go until he was buried to the hilt inside Laesa. That first, slow thrust was a taste of heaven, and once he'd felt that, he couldn't hold back any longer. He watched his brother move to the top of the bed and reach down to take one of Laesa's hands, drawing it over her head. Sabar twined their fingers so that the three of them were still connected, and the action resonated deep in Rhen's soul. The three of them together felt right. It was as if the pieces of their lives had clicked into a new formation. The duo they'd once were had been replaced by something stronger. A trio.

That was the last lucid thought to cross his mind before his need for Laesa made it impossible to think. Sensation replaced reason, and years of carefully honed control shattered as he lost himself in the glory of her body. She wrapped her long legs around his hips and met every one of his thrusts, matching him move for move. Her inner muscles gripped his dick tightly, adding to his pleasure.

Laesa let herself be swept away by passion. For the first time since her capture, she was free to be herself. When Rhen gave a low, shuddering moan, she flexed her inner walls around him, deliberately milking his cock as it powered into her. He groaned again in response, the sound rolling through her like the tolling of a bell.

Rhen's pace grew faster, his movements less measured as he neared release. Without warning, he shifted his position, changing the angle of his thrusts so that the head of his cock stroked over her sweet spot. Her breath caught in her throat as her body erupted into an orgasm that tore through her with the force of a Tarin storm. He came only a few thrusts later, her name on his lips as he emptied himself inside her.

When her mind returned, the first thing she noticed was that she was humming with energy and felt as if she'd rested for a week. It was incredible. The second thing she noticed was Rhen staring down at her with something like wonder in his amber eyes.

"You are breathtaking," he murmured. He brushed a tender kiss to her mouth before easing himself off of her to collapse onto the bed at her side.

"We are…" she trailed off, unable to find the words to express what she was feeling.

"We are, indeed." Sabar squeezed her hand, and she craned her head back to see him smiling at her.

"Did you feed? Is that something I should be asking, or is that considered rude?" Rhen asked.

She laughed before answering. "I did. Very well. I had not thought it could be like that with someone who wasn't my consort."

"It's different with a consort?" Sabar asked.

"It's different with someone we're bonded to. More intense," she explained.

"If we mate you, it will be more intense, too. We'll be linked. You'll be able to hear our thoughts," Rhen said.

"I would?" The idea intrigued her.

"Mhmm. You would. We'd bite you and leave our marks on your skin forever, telling everyone you belonged to us."

"And if we bonded, I'd share my energy with you. You'd carry part of me with you, always."

"Anytime you're ready to do that, you say the word, blossom." Sabar moved in and kissed her. "I already know that's what I want."

"I do not know how you can be so certain already."

Rhen chuckled. "We did warn you that once we have something we want, we don't let go."

"Indeed, you did. I will have to remember that in future," she said.

Her thoughts were all over the place as they took turns cleaning up and returning to bed. Eventually, all three of them were together again, with Laesa nestled snuggly between her two males. It was comforting to have them so close to her, and she tried to imagine going to sleep this way every night for the rest of her life. It seemed too good to be true. From harem slave to cherished lover was an even greater journey than the one she'd embarked on the day she'd left Tartarus.

Perhaps this had been her final destination all along.

CHAPTER FIVE

Sabar stole a kiss from Laesa as he walked her to the entrance to her small workspace. It was a ritual he'd started the first morning they'd woken up together on board the *Auranox* more than two weeks ago. They'd walk together and talk about their plans. It was one of the highlights of his day. In fact, being with Laesa had become the best part of all their days. For the first time since they'd left home, both he and Rhen were taking time for themselves. They were still working, but there was more to their lives than the next deal.

There was Laesa.

They had taken her out for meals, and she'd even braved the dark and noisy Krytos bar on several occasions, though she'd stuck close to the two of them every time. They'd enlisted Sophie's help, and bought Laesa new outfits in bright colors and flattering designs. They'd taken great joy in buying her anything and everything they could think of, and while she'd argued at first, eventually she'd given in and accepted their gifts. Now it had become something of a game, with both of them competing to see who could find the most interesting presents for their female.

A few days ago, the three of them had attended the opening ceremony of the station. It had filled Sabar with pride to be able to stand with Laesa at his side. It had made him even happier to see her move among the crowd without any hesitation or doubt. She walked with her head high and a smile on her face, wearing one of the dresses he'd chosen for her. Her confidence was growing, and so was her trust that he and Rhen would protect her from any threat. She'd proven her trust later that day.

After the ceremony, their friend, Alliance Liaison Officer Morgan D'Sil had been accosted and insulted by one of the D'Aire, Laesa hadn't so much as flinched. She'd held her ground while Sabar and his brother had intervened on Morgan's behalf. Not that the tough Alliance female needed their help, but they weren't the kind to stand by and let a friend be mistreated.

Afterward Laesa confessed to being fascinated by the D'Aire since she'd spotted several of them outside her shop a few days before. Apparently she'd wanted to see one in flight so that she could paint them properly. When D'Aire Ambassador Orion D'Sil had flown in to see to his keeper, Morgan's, wellbeing, Laesa had been too busy admiring his wings to be concerned about the violence she'd witnessed.

"I'm getting close to finishing your portraits, by the way. Another day or so, and I should be done," Laesa said, drawing his thoughts back to the here and now.

"Already? You don't need to rush, blossom. You know we're happy to wait." He and Rhen had already agreed that they weren't leaving the station without Laesa. They'd postpone their next journey for as long as it took for her to agree to come with them.

Laesa laughed. "I'm inspired. I think of you both all the time, and it helps keep me focused on my work. I'd be done already, but I had that other commission come in, and it's been taking up a fair bit of my time."

"You mean that rainbow-hued explosion of color and cuteness you've been working on? That thing is so bright it hurts my eyes every time I see it."

"It's not that bad! Well, it's a little colorful, but Commander Jacobson was very clear about what she wanted." She giggled, her eyes dancing with mirth.

"I can't wait for that reveal. We're going to hear the bellows all over the station when those Krytos brothers see what she's bought them. Not that you haven't done a great job of it, but it's so big and...cheerful."

"Wait until you see the puppies I'm adding."

"There are puppies now?"

She nodded, still giggling.

"Stars. That's going to be a hell of a reveal. You know that's not the artwork I'm keen to see finished, though. I can't wait to get a look at the ones of Rhen and I. I'm a big fan of the artist, you see," he told her with a grin and a wink.

"I happen to know that the artist is very fond of you, too," she said.

He pulled her back into his arms for another kiss. "I'm glad to hear that. As it happens, I'm not fond of you anymore. I'm falling in love with you. When you think of me today, remember that."

She stared at him wide-eyed for a moment before speaking. "I—I will. You really love me?"

"I really do. I've never said those words to any other female, and I don't expect I ever will again. Someday, soon I hope, I know you're going to agree to be our companion. We're meant to be."

She smiled at him with tears sparkling on her dark lashes. "I never expected this. You. The two of you. I never believed I could be this happy. But I am. I'm so happy it scares me because I don't want it to end."

"This isn't going to end. This is only the beginning," he told her.

"I love it when you say things like that," she said before kissing him softly and leaving the circle of his arms.

Laesa had never been so happy, or so terrified. Every night she drifted off to sleep feeling safe and cherished, and every morning, she would wake convinced that her time with them had only been a dream. Joy and love were not things she'd ever expected to feel again, but she was coming to believe that the three of them truly were destined to be together. The shadows of her old life were falling away, and every day that passed, she fell a little more in love with Rhen and Sabar.

"You're doing touch-ups on Sophie's mural today, aren't you?" Sabar asked, changing the subject.

"I am. I need to redo part of the first section. For some reason, the paint cracked and the colors faded a little. Sophie insists it's fine, but I know it could be better, and I want it perfect before I leave—whenever that may be."

"Say the word, and we'll be on our way," he said with a wink and a smile that made her heart beat a little faster.

"Soon. But not today. I have one more portrait to finish before I go anywhere. I promised Sophie one for her to give to her bonded on their anniversary."

He caught her hand and kissed her fingers. "Soon, huh? I like the sound of that. I'll see you for lunch, blossom. Rhen's buying today, so tell Sophie I'll take two of everything on the menu."

"I'll let her know," she said with a laugh before heading inside. It would take her several hours to remove the damaged paint, prepare the surface, and redo the area she wasn't happy with. With any luck, she should be done by the time the lunch rush arrived at the café, along with Rhen and Sabar, who had adopted Sophie and her restaurant as something of a second home.

It took a little longer than Laesa had planned to redo the mural that covered an entire wall of Sophie's restaurant. The concept had been Sophie's, and the two of them had worked together to ensure that the mural melded into the color and style of the café. It was a warm, welcoming space meant to set people at ease as they enjoyed carefully prepared fare that was all made from scratch each day.

The mural started with a scene from Earth, showing a stretch of mountains that reached into an azure sky. As the picture went on, the scenery changed, each segment blending into the one beside it until there was a recognizable image from the home world of all of the Alliance's allies. Helix, Arcadia, D'Aire, Reema, and finally Tartarus. Because the Krytos home world had been destroyed by the same vile alien race that had nearly wiped out Earth, she hadn't been able to include a Krytos landscape. Instead, she'd finished the mural with an image of Asylum's sign and doors welcoming patrons to the Krytos sanctuary onboard X21.

. It was the Earth portion that needed reworking, which meant that Laesa was near the front of the café, her back to the door as she worked on the lower corner.

Sophie's bonded, Dan and Jake, were the reason it was taking her longer to finish than Laesa had initially intended. The two Alliance officers were both off-duty and spending the day with their chosen, and Laesa found herself drawn into their conversations time and again. Even when she was silent, it was easy to let her attention stray back to the bonded trio as they enjoyed each other's company. There was such love between them it was hard to turn away. The three of them laughed and teased each other as Sophie organized herself and her staff. From time to time, one of her males would try to help, and she would invariably chase them out of the kitchen and back to their seat.

As she worked, Laesa remembered similar times from her childhood. Times when her parents had laughed and talked at the end of a day with the family together and happy. She hadn't allowed herself to dwell on those memories since they'd died. In the beginning, there had been no time to grieve for them or for herself. It had taken all she had to adapt to her new circumstances. She'd seen others refuse to accept what had happened to them. She'd watched as they had been punished and threatened until either their spirit or their bodies broke.

She'd been lost in her thoughts for a while before it dawned on her that she recalled those dark times without tears or anger overwhelming her. The grief of all she'd lost was still there, but somehow, the weight of it had become less than it had been. She was healing, and she knew that it was because of more than her new life and her pursuit of her art.

It was because of Sabar and Rhen. They'd brought joy and love back into her life. Once again she found herself looking over at Dan, Jake, and Sophie as they laughed together and the truth of what she wanted hit her with all the force of a runaway comet. She wanted what Sophie had, and all she had to do to make it happen was to say yes.

She was so distracted by her revelation that when her wrist unit chimed with an incoming call, she answered it without thinking. She expected it to be Rhen or Sabar, but instead, it was another familiar face that appeared on her monitor.

"How do you fare, Laesa? I'm pleased that you've finally chosen to speak with me."

"Nevhar? Why are you calling me?"

Her father's oldest friend had a disapproving scowl on his face, and it took her a moment to realize it was because she'd let her annoyance show. Nevhar expected the females around him to be respectful and submissive at all times.

"I am calling because I was worried about you. You have not answered any of my messages. I was concerned for your wellbeing."

"I am well. I did not feel it necessary to reply to your messages because they all said the same thing, and you already had my answer to the question you continue to ask of me. While I appreciate your offer, I am never returning to Tartarus." Laesa met the older male's gaze squarely, and reminded herself that she was a free citizen. She didn't have to answer to Nevhar or anyone else. Not anymore.

He sighed. "This stubbornness does not become you. As I explained to you before you left, you are much too lovely and gentle to go about your life without someone to protect you. I can offer you so much, little Laesa. It's time for you to come home and take your place in my household."

"Tartarus is no longer my home. I thought I made that clear to you. Your offer, while generous, is not something I will ever be interested in. My life is my own now."

"Laesa, is everything okay?" Sophie asked. Laesa turned to find her friend and her two bonded standing not far away, their faces full of concern.

She nodded briefly and gave Sophie a brief smile. "I am fine. The caller is Nevhar Antor, a friend of my father. He is worried about my wellbeing, but now that I have made it clear that there is nothing for him to be concerned about, he should not be contacting me again."

Nevhar's scowl deepened, his eyes glittering with barely checked anger. "You need to stop this foolishness and return to Tartarus. I would keep you safe to honor your parents' memories. It is what they would want for you."

"I'm not returning, Nevhar. Nor do I need your protection. My life is my own, and I will live it however I choose. I think my parents would be proud of me for what I have accomplished." Speaking to Nevhar reminded her why she'd left her home world. Males like him were resistant to the changes coming to Tartarus. If she returned to him, she would give up so much of her freedom in exchange for his promised protection that it would be as if she were still a harem slave.

"I think it would break your father's heart to see what has become of you."

Laesa stared at the monitor for a second, too stunned by his cruel words to speak. When she spoke again, she barely recognized the voice as her own. "You're wrong. I have found the males I wish to be with. Males who are honorable, kind, and loving. I have a life, and it is not, and never will be with you. I never wish to hear from you again. My answer is as it always was. No. "

She deactivated the link with a flick of her finger. "Thundersfury, he had no right to say such a thing about my father."

"Did you just curse? You did! Damn, honey, I never thought I'd see the day." Sophie was grinning at her.

"I think that was the sexiest thing you've ever done. I like the way you cut him off, too."

Sabar spoke from somewhere behind her, and she spun around to find herself being pulled into his arms. "Hello, blossom. Who was that, and do we have your permission to kill him for talking to you that way?"

"Hello, Sabar. That was someone I hope never to hear from again. If I do, you and Rhen have my permission to tell him that I am very well protected by two big, sexy males."

"Are you okay, love? That sounded…intense," Rhen asked.

"I'm fine. Speaking to him only reminded me of all the reasons I left Tartarus. My life is out here now. In fact, I was thinking about you before he interrupted. I was painting the mural and then I realized—and I was going to tell you that I knew what I wanted. But then he called—and now here you are." She laughed when she heard the tangle of words coming out of her mouth.

Rhen tapped a point behind his ear. "Want to say that again? Not even my language converter could make sense of what you said."

Laesa waved her hands in front of her. "None of that matters. All that matters is this. My answer is yes."

"Yes?" Sabar repeated, his arms tightening around her.

"Yes, yes, yes," she repeated herself several times over as she threw her arms around Sabar's neck.

Sophie cheered. "It's about damned time, too."

Rhen brushed his knuckles down her cheek and marveled that the beauty in his brother's arms was going to be theirs. Always. "I'm glad to hear it." Then he turned his attention to Sophie and her grinning men. "It appears we have somewhere else to be right now. Sorry, Sophie. We'll be back for lunch…tomorrow."

Sabar took one of her hands while Rhen snagged the other and made eye contact with his brother. They both started back toward the ship at the same time, taking Laesa with them. Now that she'd said yes there was only one thing on their minds. Claiming her as their companion and binding their lives together forever.

"I'll finish the mural later. Can you lock up for me? Thanks, Sophie and uh…bye!" Laesa called out to her friend as they left.

"I'd apologize for rushing you out of there, but I'm not at all sorry," Rhen said.

"Same here," Sabar agreed.

"Are you going to tell me where we're going in such a hurry?" Laesa asked.

"Home. And none of us are leaving again until we're claimed, life-locked, marked, and whatever else is required to make the three of us a permanent trio."

Laesa laughed, the joyful sound loud enough to make everyone within earshot turn in their direction. "Then take me home, my beloveds. There's nowhere else I'd rather be."

Rhen's heart soared when he heard her call them her beloveds. It was the first time she'd called them any kind of endearment. She had finally accepted what he and Sabar already knew. The three of them were meant for each other.

The walk across the station felt like it took an age to complete. The moment the *Auranox*'s door opened, the three of them rushed inside, getting tangled up with each other in their haste.

"Sirs? I understood that you would be having lunch with Laesa—Oh, hello, Laesa. I gather there was a change in plans?" Ashar was standing a few feet away, an expression of bemusement on his face.

"Change in plans. Yes. A big one," Sabar said, wrapping his arms around Laesa.

"We'll be eating in. For the next few meals, in fact. Please let Jonah know," Rhen requested, hoping their long-suffering assistant got the message and got out of their way.

"I see. Since you're here, I've got an update on that very special order you've been working on. Would you like the long version or the short one?" Ashar asked, and Rhen could have sworn he was making them wait on purpose.

"The very fucking short version, please," Rhen snapped.

"I called in a few favors and tracked down a sufficient amount of the Nexerion coffee beans. They are already on their way here, and will arrive tomorrow. You're welcome. I know I'm incredible, and yes, I deserve a raise."

"Ashar, you're incredible, thank you, and if you don't get out of our way in the next three seconds you're going to be looking for a new career," Sabar said, his voice bordering on a snarl.

"Forgive them, Ashar. I've just agreed to be their companion, and they're in a hurry to make it official," Laesa explained.

Ashar's eyes widened, and he grinned wide enough to show his fangs. "Is that so? Well then, let me be the first to congratulate you. And now, I'll get out of your way."

"Why, thank you, Ashar." Sabar's droll response had Laesa giggling.

"All you had to do was tell me why you were in such a hurry, sir," Ashar said as he stepped aside.

"Why do we keep him around?" Sabar grumbled as they headed toward their quarters.

"Because I'm amazing, not to mention I'm the only one you've ever found who will put up with the two of you. Laesa, I wish you luck. You're going to need it." Ashar said, then turned and headed in the other direction before Rhen could do more than growl.

"I like him," Laesa announced.

"In that case, he's absolutely fired," Rhen said, only half-joking.

"Right out an airlock," Sabar agreed.

"I mean he's sweet and bratty. Like a little brother. I am not looking to add anyone else to this relationship. The two of you are more than enough for me." Laesa turned and offered them a smile that left no doubt as to her feelings. Her love for them glowed like an inner fire.

"Damn right. We're all you're ever going to need, blossom." Sabar led the way down the corridor, passing the doors to both their quarters until he arrived at a door at the end of the passageway.

"Where are we going, now?" Laesa asked. As far as she knew, there were only offices and guest berths this far down.

"Your quarters," Sabar said as he opened the door and led her inside.

Laesa looked around her in stunned silence. The main room was spacious and opulently decorated. The bed was larger than her entire room on the station, and the bedspread seemed to shimmer and shift colors as she moved closer. There were soft rugs in bright colors covering the floor, and more of the wonderful, ever-changing fabric draped the walls to create an inviting bower.

"Welcome home. The bathing area is through that door, and the door to your new studio is there," Rhen said. He came up behind her to set a hand on her shoulder as she stood and tried to take it all in.

"Why?" There were tears in her eyes as she crossed to the bed and stroked a hand over the exquisitely soft bedspread. "What is this? It's beautiful. It's all so beautiful."

"The fabric is made on Helix. It's called *saedea,* and it's one of the first things we brought with us when we started out as traders. As for why—we wanted to make this place match its owner. We wanted to make it as lovely as you are." Sabar said.

Rhen pressed a kiss to the side of her throat. "Do you like it?"

She was so overwhelmed she didn't know where to begin answering that question. "I love it. I cannot believe you did this for me. What if I didn't say yes?"

Sabar raised one brow and threw his arms out wide. "Of course you were going to say yes. There was never any doubt in our minds. We're amazing, and we knew eventually you'd figure that out."

"Ignore him. What he meant to say was that we're utterly in love with you, and hoped that you'd come to feel the same way about us," Rhen said.

Laesa turned from the bed to smile at Rhen. "I do love you. I love you both, and I want us to be together. I realized today that I'm finally free of my past. What happened doesn't haunt me anymore. Everything I do from now on is my choice, and I choose to be with the two of you."

"I want forever with you, Laesa Fen," Rhen murmured before kissing her with a passion that left no room for doubt.

"As do I," Sabar said as he moved in behind her.

They undressed between kisses until there was a pile of clothing on the floor, and the three of them were skin to skin. They had her caught between them, mouths and hands caressing and tasting every part of her they could reach. When she was breathless and dizzy with need, they guided her to the bed, coaxing her to kneel between them as they continued their assault on her senses.

Sabar was behind her, hands on her hips and the heavy length of his cock pressed against her back as he left a trail of fiery kisses up the side of her neck. Rhen knelt in front of her, his hands cupping her breasts as he kissed and nuzzled his way down her throat on the opposite side from his brother.

"I love you," Rhen whispered as he raked his fangs across her skin.

"You're ours, my love," Sabar whispered.

Two sets of fangs sank into her flesh a second later. It didn't hurt as much as she'd expected. Instead of pain, there was a flare of heat followed by a rush of intense pleasure. They'd claimed her for their own.

Rhen released her first, raising his head to stare down at her with such satisfaction that she blushed.

"Mine," he said before slanting a hard kiss across her lips.

She tasted the metallic tang of blood as their mouths met, and she knew what he'd done. An exchange of blood was needed to form the life-lock between them. He'd tasted her blood and now she'd tasted his. It was done.

Sabar kissed her next, but before he did, he let her watch as he deliberately bit his lower lip until a drop of blood welled up from the cut. She kissed him eagerly, wanting to seal the link between them as well. They'd explained to her that once they'd claimed her this way, she would be able to speak with them telepathically, but nothing felt different.

"Is that it? Maybe it didn't work," she muttered.

"Patience, blossom. Give it a minute or two. If that's what you're thinking about right now, then I believe Rhen and I need to be working harder to keep your interest."

Before she could say a word, Laesa found herself tumbled onto her back looking up at identical grins.

"Hello, companion. I have to say you look even more beautiful now you're wearing our marks on your throat," Rhen said.

"Very sexy," Sabar agreed.

"I want to see them," she said, brushing a finger over the still tender spots on her throat.

"Soon. But I'm not letting you out of this bed until we're your bonded consorts. We've claimed you as our own, now you get to return the favor." Rhen told her.

"Mine," Sabar whispered and ran a hand down her naked flank, his heart full, and his cock aching as he thought of what was to come.

"Ours. Open your legs for me, Laesa. I need to taste you, first," Rhen said.

She parted her thighs, and Sabar watched as his brother moved into position in seconds, growling low in his throat as he buried his face in her pussy.

Soft moans of pleasure filled the air as Rhen pleasured their female. Sabar knew this was where he wanted to be every night for the rest of his life. Laesa belonged to them now, and they would never give her any reason to regret her decision to link her life to theirs.

He stroked his cock as he watched Laesa writhe and buck on the bed. She was beautiful this way. Her face was flushed with passion, her lips parted, and her fingers tangled into the bedspread beneath her. Her scent surrounded him even now, and he could still taste her blood on his tongue. As she came undone, her wordless cries were sweet music to his ears. Their beautiful companion was a feast for the senses, one he intended to indulge in for the rest of his life.

Laesa was still trembling with the aftershocks of her release when Rhen gathered her into his arms and rolled them both over so that she was on top of him, her body draped across his. She glanced over at Sabar to find him watching them with heat blazing in his golden eyes as he stroked his erection with a slow and practiced hand. In the days since she'd come to their bed, she'd discovered that both brothers enjoyed watching her with the other one, and as time passed, she'd learned that she liked to be watched. It was empowering to know that she could arouse and tempt them without so much as a single caress.

She lowered her head to Rhen's, brushing a kiss across his mouth as she settled her body over his, straddling him so that his cock was pressed against the seam of her pussy. The contact made Rhen groan, and he arched his hips, rubbing himself against her swollen clit. She reached between them and guided the thick head of his cock to her entrance. As she eased herself down over his shaft, she laid her other hand on his chest over his heart, and whispered, "I love you."

Rhen looked back at her with eyes full of love. She opened herself to him, drinking in his energy as she started to move in time to the music of her heart. As his essence flowed into her, she felt his presence growing in her mind. Their connection grew stronger with every passing second. She rode him hard, his cock pounding into her as she let go of everything but the pleasure of the moment. He was inside her head and her heart, as well as her body, both of them caught up in a storm of passion.

At the moment of her release, she directed the sexual energy within her back to Rhen. It flowed through her hand and into his heart, filling him with a part of herself just as he exploded into orgasm.

"Mine. Always." His voice filled her head.

"Yes, you are," she answered back the same way. There were tears on her cheeks as she leaned down and kissed Rhen again. "All mine."

Sabar cleared his throat. "So, did it work? I've got to point out that the Helios way is a lot more obvious than whatever you two just did."

"Our way may be more obvious, but believe me, brother; Laesa's way has its own appeal. Holy nova, does it ever." Rhen muttered, cracking open one eye to look up at her.

"Do you need to rest before doing it again?" Sabar asked.

Laesa shook her head, laughing. "Rest? Stars no, I do not need to rest. I've never felt so energized in my life!"

"Then come here and let me love you, blossom."

The moment she came into Sabar's arms he claimed her mouth with his. Need drove him hard, one kiss leading to another as he laid her down and covered her body with his own. She wrapped her long legs around his hips, pulling him in close. Her fingers tangled in his hair and she laughed as they came together, a joyful sound that became a moan of need as his cock found her entrance and slid inside.

He lost himself in the slick heat of her body, his need for her overwhelming every other thought. Her inner walls gripped his cock, battering at his control until it shattered. As he drove himself deep into her body, she placed her hand over his heart and unleashed a flood of energy so powerful he felt as if he'd fallen into the heart of a thunderstorm. Laesa's voice was inside his head as part of all she was flowed into him. Her essence filled his heart and overflowed his soul. Energy surged through him and he came harder than he'd ever done before. It took a while for the storm to pass, but when it did, he could still hear her voice whispering inside his mind.

"*I love you, Sabar.*"

"*And I, you. Forever.*"

As he came back to his senses, Sabar brushed a tender kiss to his companion's smiling lips. "Now I understand what Rhen meant about your way having its own appeal. That was incredible."

She cupped his cheek tenderly and gave him a look of pure devotion. "For me as well. We're truly joined now. I never imagined I could be this happy."

Rhen reached out and took Laesa's free hand in his. "You make us happy, too. You're what was missing from our life."

Laesa beamed at them both. "And now that I have you, I'm not ever going to let you go."

SUSAN HAYES

EPILOGUE

Laesa sat at her easel with a paintbrush in her hand, capturing the details of the holographic scene laid out in front of her. Birds sang in the distance, and the thick blue-green grass of Helix was soft beneath her bare feet. The breeze that blew around her was warm and scented with the delicate scent of the wild flowers that grew in the meadow she was currently painting.

"When you said you wanted to paint us naked, this wasn't what I had in mind," Rhen grumbled inside her head.

"I'll be done soon. I only hope your parents like it," she said aloud. Glancing up from her work, she looked over at her consorts. They were both in their animal form, two massive creatures posed so that the sun struck their golden fur perfectly. They were both looking at her with mild annoyance in their amber eyes, and she knew it was time to stop.

"You said soon more than an hour ago, blossom."

"Did I lose track of time again?" She glanced at her wrist unit and winced as she saw the time. "Oops. Okay, you're free to move."

Both of them shook themselves and stretched, their big bodies arching as their claws dug into the grass. Rhen yawned, his deadly fangs flashing in the sun. She loved seeing them this way. They were breathtaking in their feline forms, all power and deadly grace. Sabar padded over to her and pushed his broad head into her lap with a low, rumbling purr. She buried her hands in his fur, stroking his head and ears as the starburst-shaped scars he'd left on her throat began to heat and tingle. It had been strange at first, but she was slowly getting used to the way her body reacted when her consorts were close by.

"I'm sorry I made you sit still so long. Would you like to see what I've done?" she asked.

Rhen shook himself and came over to sit on her other side, and his claiming marks reacted to his presence as well. She set a hand on her lover's head and all three of them looked at the painting she'd been working on. It was to be a gift for her new family when they arrived on Helix in a matter of days. Her consorts had insisted that no gift was needed, but she wanted to be able to give them something that came from her heart. After all, they were her family now. They were even hosting a party to celebrate their mating.

"*They're going to love it,*" Rhen told her.

"*Damn, I look good,*" Sabar said.

"If you two turn back to your other forms, this conversation would be much simpler," she said as both their voices sounded in her mind at the same time.

They shifted back as she watched. It still amazed her to see the transformation take place, and she suspected it always would.

"Next time you paint us, I vote we're all naked," Sabar said.

"As I recall, the last time we tried that, I didn't actually get any painting done at all," she replied.

"Exactly my point." Sabar reached up to tweak the laces that held her leather vest closed.

She'd taken to wearing some Helios-style clothing. It was surprisingly comfortable, and the reaction of her males the first time she'd appeared bare-armed and clothed in leather pants had been more than enough incentive for her to wear it more often.

"What if I don't want to be naked right now?" she asked, playfully swatting Sabar's hand from her laces.

"Then you should have probably chosen two other males to be your companions. We like you to be naked as often as possible," Rhen said.

"Hmm. You have a point. In that case, you can have me naked, but only if you can catch me." With a whoop of joy, Laesa sprang from her chair and started racing across the meadow.

"Cheater!" Sabar howled in protest as he took off after her with his brother only a half-step behind.

"Like I was going to let you chase me when you both had four legs instead of two!" she shot back over her shoulder. Not that it would make any difference in the end. Her consorts were warriors, far stronger and faster than she would ever be. And that was one of the many reasons she loved them. They were her strength, and in return she was their joy. Together, they were a family who made their home among the stars.

Wherever Rhen and Sabar were, that was her home.

—⊖—

ABOUT THE AUTHOR

Susan lives out on the Canadian west coast surrounded by open water, dear family, and good friends. She's jumped out of perfectly good airplanes on purpose and accidently swum with sharks on the Great Barrier Reef.

She's worked for local law enforcement, been a freelance wordsmith and bakes what she claims are the world's best double-chocolate & caramel brownies. She's passionately in love with the written word (and a few of her more hunky creations.) Writing is her joy, her escape from reality and the only way she knows of to quiet the nagging harridan of a muse the universe assigned to her.

Susan loves to hear from her readers. You can contact her at susanhayesromance@gmail.com.

For all titles by Susan Hayes, please visit
SusanHayes.ca

3013: THE SERIES
http://3013theseries.blogspot.com